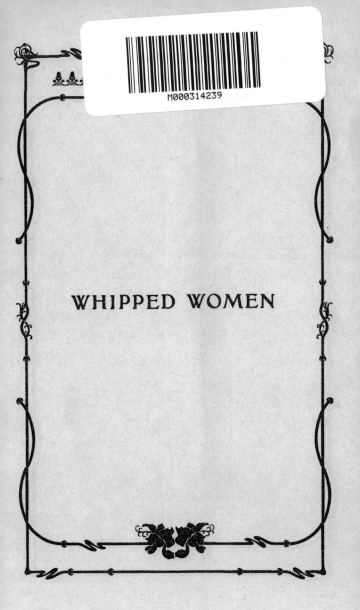

WHIPPED WOMEN

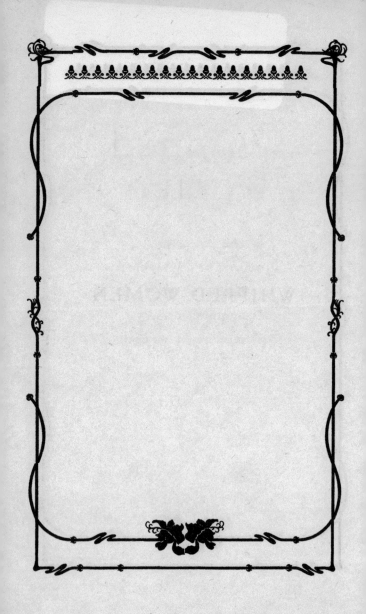

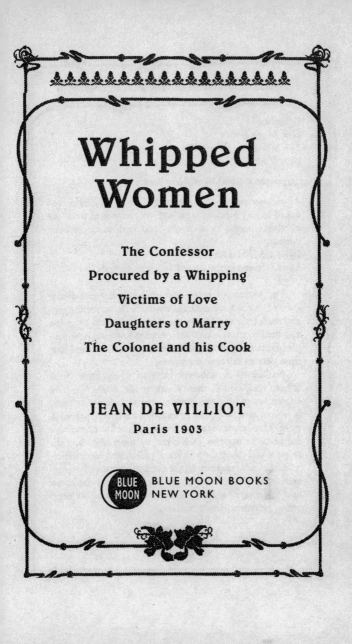

Whipped Women

The Confessor
Procured by a Whipping
Victims of Love
Daughters to Marry
The Colonel and his Cook

JEAN DE VILLIOT
Paris 1903

BLUE MOON BOOKS
NEW YORK

Published by
Blue Moon Books
841 Broadway, Fourth Floor
New York, NY 10003

ISBN 1-56201-190-1
Manufactured in the United States of America

The history of erotic literature is long and distin-
guished. It holds valuable lessons and insights for the general reader, the sociologist, the student of sexual behavior,
and the literary specialist interested in knowing how people of different cultures and different times acted and how
these actions relate to the present.

Because of the inherent value to all students of the
human condition of these classic erotic works, we have
chosen not to alter this book in any way, shape, or form.
It is presented to the reader exactly as it first appeared in
print. Thus, all of the subtleties are exposed to our view—
the haste or extreme care taken by the author and the
original publisher, the manner of speech and communication, the colloquialisms of the time, the means of expression, and the concepts of erotic stimulation—both real
and imaginary—used by the writer who was, in every
sense, representative of his time.

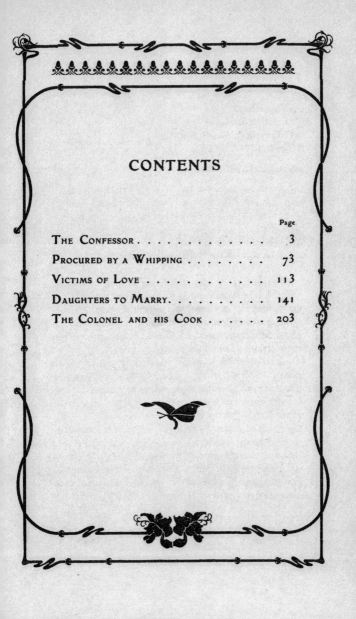

CONTENTS

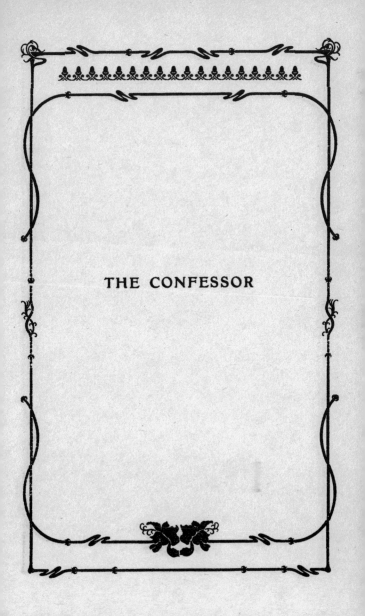

THE CONFESSOR

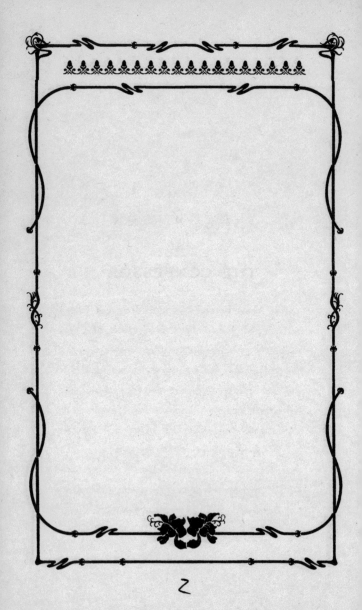

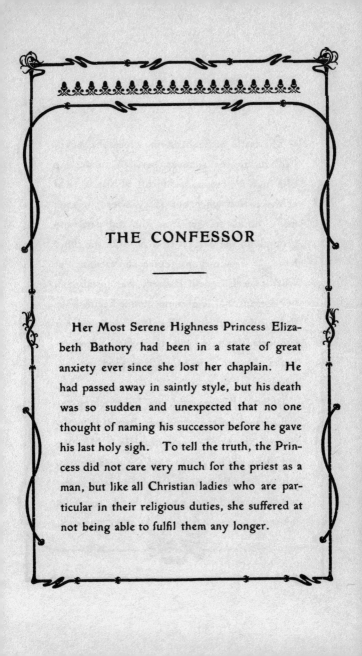

THE CONFESSOR

Her Most Serene Highness Princess Elizabeth Bathory had been in a state of great anxiety ever since she lost her chaplain. He had passed away in saintly style, but his death was so sudden and unexpected that no one thought of naming his successor before he gave his last holy sigh. To tell the truth, the Princess did not care very much for the priest as a man, but like all Christian ladies who are particular in their religious duties, she suffered at not being able to fulfil them any longer.

The castle of Seebenstein, which she inhabited during the summer, perched on the top
of a high mountain, is difficult of access; and
at the period when our story opens, it took
many hours to get from the old park and
grounds to the nearest church. On the other
hand, it was easy to return to Vienna, but
when once Elizabeth Bathory was installed in
her domain, nothing could induce her to leave
it until the autumn. The Princess loved her
comforts, laziness, and every kind of voluptuous pleasure quite as much as God and religion.

Before attending mass and approaching the
consecrated host, she resigned herself to awaiting the arrival of a new chaplain. Morning
and night she prayed to God for the advent of
a holy man. Sometimes she did so with tears,
as she regretted having no one handy to whom
she could confess her faults. At other moments,

she was seized with violent fury because her prayers were not granted, so she beat her serving women and exhausted her rage on the shoulders and thighs of her vassals. The Princess being in all the glory of blossoming youth; so perfectly well-built, having such a seductive face and magnificent and liberal ways, that her brutality was supported without too much grumbling, but as her maids thought they knew the reason of her temper, they tried at any rate to moderate and restrain her capricious cruelty, being unable to escape from it entirely. Refusing to trust in Providence alone, they informed everybody serving in the castle, of their mistress's new whim, begging them, if they should be passing through Vienna to find out some unattached priest who would be agreeable to come and take up his abode at Seebenstein. The post was well and amply paid, and the wenches added that if necessary, they would pay the priest's salary out of their wages.

But the man was finally found, and one rainy evening when the Princess had shown herself particularly cross and hasty, a certain Abbot of the name of Thurzo came knocking at the castle gates. He wore a long beard like a missionary; his hair was growing grey, and tinted spectacles protected his eyes. But these were the only signs of age. Being tall, straight, and well set-up, with fine ruddy cheeks and broad shoulders, everything pointed on the contrary to full strength and fine bodily health, so that if he was no longer a young man, at any rate he carried the burden of old age lightly enough.

Elizabeth Bathory, to whom the arrival of the priest had been promptly announced, received him with the most exquisite welcome, and Ursula, one of her maids, was entrusted with the care of showing him to his new apartments, in order that he could attend to his dress before going to take supper. He had to dwell rather far away from the lady of the manor, in a part of the building opposite the wing occupied by Elizabeth, so therefore, as he made his way in the ante-chamber of his quarters, Ursula, after glancing back over her shoulder, thought she could safely give him the following strange warning :

" My lord Abbot, " she exclaimed, " tarry not in the castle of Seebenstein, if thou wouldst not die like our venerable chaplain ! "

" What was the manner of his demise ? " asked the priest.

" He succumbed beneath the blows of the Princess, " replied Ursula, in low tones, as if she was affrighted at having let this avowal escape her. Hearing a slight noise at the end of the corridor, she made haste to light some tapers, and putting in order the three rooms which for two centuries had been set aside for the chaplains of Seebenstein, made a precipitate exit.

The holy man did not appear to be much stirred by Ursula's discourse.

" Whatever befall, " he muttered between his clenched teeth, " I am not the sort of man to die under the blows of this woman ! "

He quietly arranged his dress, and was about to leave his apartment, when he caught sight of a large brown stain on the wooden flooring. On the naked wall was another spot, and this one was in the shape of a hand. There could be no doubt about it : fingers with strong nails had scratched and drawn lines on the stuccoed surface. The priest felt momentary astonishment, but the sound of the supper-bell left him no time to give way to his thoughts.

The mistress of the house was seated at table

between a rather tall girl and a very young woman. At one moment, the Princess would treat her like an intimate friend, and afterwards with the sort of condescending authority that one might have for quite a baby lassie. By the jovial vivacity of their talk and bearing, all three harmonized but little with this vast dull hall, only ornamented with antlers, hunting horns and weapons, together with some heads of wild boars and a few sombre portraits of ancestors, whose sour looks seemed to grow worse at the sight of the supple, naked, fair, brilliant, transparent shoulders, all ablaze with diamonds; and the magnificent yellow tresses arranged by the hands of expert Viennese artists. Beneath the illuminating glare of the chandeliers, it seemed as if three heavy golden diadems were surmounting their swan-like necks. The surly old bygone Bathorys would certainly become more crabbed in the face of their enchanting cruppers, standing out in such high relief that the silky skirts of gala clothing seemed rather to enhance than to hide them. These widely spreading and majestuous hemispheres could be easily viewed between the backs and cushions of the heavy armchairs : cruppers large and vast were they, of indolent, sovereign queens ; firm, rounded, moon-like cruppers of intrepid amazons ; jutting, tight-skinned cruppers—the immodest rotundities of voluptuous and rakish females.

Princess Bathory, since her father's death, had evidently not had time to substitute more modern furniture for the old appointments of the castle. She required something more in accordance with her own tastes ; or mayhap she was too occupied by the ardent life of passionate sensuality she led to pay much attention to tables and chairs.

The Princess introduced Abbot Thurzo to

her two neighbours at table, Lenchen and Adelgonda, her two cousins. The three young ladies began to question the priest concerning the clergy and society in Vienna, seemingly wanting to find out what kind of people he had known, and his intellectual value. By his replies it could be seen that he had moved in the highest circles. All three of the women made disparaging remarks about their female friends, trying to get him to talk scandal, but he eluded the snare by clever witticisms.

" If Madame Nadardy has ever been in your company, " said young Lenchen, towards the end of the meal, " I think she must have enticed you into her boudoir. "

" Whatever do you mean ? " asked the Princess, throwing up her head, and in a severe tone of voice, as she turned to Lenchen, on her right.

" Only just for a little private chat, " continued pretty Lenchen, without noticing her cousin's irritation, and she added with a half comical, half voluptuous expression, " see what a fine beard the Abbot has ! "

" What means such chatter ? " exclaimed the Princess, and she twice slapped the cheeks of Lenchen, who to protect herself, rapidly threw up her elbow. This quick gesture caused her involuntarily to knock over a dish full of pastry that Ursula was bringing in. The cakes slid all over the carpet, and some fell upon the Princess's dress.

" Clumsy fool ! " cried Elizabeth, as she started up in a furious rage, and kicked the backside of Ursula, who had stooped to repair her awkwardness, and thus offered a target which was quite alluring. The Princess continued to beat and scold the serving maid for many minutes more. At last, she calmed down, while Ursula wept, groaned, and rubbed her hinder parts.

" Begone, whimperer ! " the Princess shouted, as she pounded on the table with her fist. " By my faith, considering that this is the way in which all these wenches behave, they deserve that I should have them whipped. "

" Why not do so, dearest ? " replied Adelgonda. " It would amuse us, and I am sure the Abbot would not find such chastisement useless, nor tiresome to look upon. Do you not agree with me, my lord Abbot ? But where is he ? "

" Yes ! Where is he ? " echoed the Princess.

" The Abbot, " said one of the ladies' maids, " left the table at the very moment your Highness was beating Ursula. "

" Oho ! Perhaps he feels sympathy with this minx ? "

" Perchance he does not like to see maid servants thus beaten. "

" Then he may leave the castle, for I do not find that gentleness is good for governing a household. Meanwhile, I have a wish to see him. I will see him, do you hear? He must come hither to me. Bring him here by main force, and at once. You hearken to me, Grethe and Jettchen ! "

The two serving girls left the hall, and remained so long absent that the Princess grew uneasy.

" What can they be about? Think you that our confessor has so forgot himself as to take indecent liberties with these girls ? "

" Just now you boxed poor Lenchen's ears, " remarked Adelgonda, " because she lacked respect for our Abbot, but methinks you are following her lead at present. "

" My dear girl, " rejoined the Princess, " he is not with us ; thus we can speak of him at our ease. Moreover, I may tell you that

I respect his vestment, but I am not bound to venerate his personality, whose qualities are unknown to me."

" How superstitious you are, dear ! "

" Oh ! you are a heathen ! "

" But perhaps less impious than you. You take a fancy to certain devotions ; but have you religious feelings ? That is what I ask myself. You give way to your temper with ferocity that affrights me. That might be excusable if you showed repentance. "

" You cannot tell whether I repent or not. The simple truth is that I have a violent disposition, which is difficult for me to moderate. But you often set down to passionate fury what is but a tendency to exact obedience and the will to repress—in short, nothing but what is quite reasonable. "

" Was it reasonable to buffet Lenchen's cheeks ? "

" The girl deserved it.   See how quiet she is now. "

That was true, for Lenchen, her cheeks scarlet, and with swollen lids, did not dare lift her eyes off her plate.

The Princess glanced at her with satisfaction, and smiled.

" And what about luckless Ursula ? " continued Adelgonda.

" She is mutinous, " said the Princess, " and I am taming her ! "

" You will kill her one of these days ! "

" My dear, did I listen to you, I should get no one to obey me.   Besides, you are cruel too."

" How could I learn to be softhearted in your company ? You are ferocious, by premeditation, refinement, and instinct. "

" How now !   You hold a good opinion of me. "

" But I love thee none the less, dear heart, "

said Adelgonda, as she kissed the naked breast of the Princess. She in return, passed her hand over her imposing foundations, pressing Adelgonda's posteriors lovingly.

" But what are my maids about ? " exclaimed Elizabeth. " Aha ! at last ! " she added, seeing the couple re-enter the dining hall. " Why are you so tardy ? "

" We begged my lord Abbot to come, " said Grethe.

" You were not to supplicate, but to order him hither. "

" He won't, " replied Jettchen.

" What mean you—he won't ? "

" He says that he will wait until your Highness goes and visits him in his apartment. "

" Then he will have wait a very long while ! "

" The boor ! " said Adelgonda. " He deserves a lesson. "

" Suppose I went to see him all the same ? "

rejoined the Princess, hesitatingly, as she seemed to consult her friend. " This eccentric fellow puzzles me. "

" Dearest, go not to him, you will dishonour yourself in his eyes. "

" No, no ! I will go ! " she cried, as she rose. " I shall have some fun. I will tell you all about it. "

She arrived at the Abbot's quarters, merrily laughing and quite at her ease.

" Well now, my dear lord Abbot, whatever is the matter ? "

Then she perceived that the Abbot was seated in an easy chair, and was touched to the quick that he had not risen to greet her, but there were more surprises in store.

" Shut the door, " he said. " It is not seemly that we should be overheard. "

When, after a moment's hesitation, she had obeyed this order, he said :

" Madam, you ought to understand how astonished I am to find that on the very night of my arrival, you allow me to be the witness of such violent outbursts and assaults. "

" My lord Abbot, " replied the Princess, quite confused, " I assure you that sometimes severity is needed for young girls and serving wenches. "

" In all that took place just now there was no severity, but rage and wickedness quite unworthy of you. Be perfectly sure that I shall never show myself again in your company unless you promise to be, at least in my presence, more tender ; calmer, and mistress of your passions. "

The Princess gave an angry toss of her proud head, and asked herself if she ought not to have such an eccentric chaplain kicked out of the Seebenstein gates, but the priest's fixed, coldly authoritative glance overawed her.

" I promise, " she said, hesitatingly, and as if in spite of herself.

" I am willing to believe you, " he replied, " but having erred, you must be punished. Come nearer. "

The Princess approached slowly, still under the domination of the priest's glance, subjugated by his will-power, so much stronger than her's, and which she felt weighed her down.

" On your knees ! " he ordered.

There was no cushion, nor carpet, and it was with extreme anxiety that Elizabeth Bathory asked herself inwardly what she ought to do and if it would not have been proper for her to resist such fantastical commands, when Thurzo the Abbot drew her close to him with humiliating familiarity, and pressing his hands on the Princess's shoulders, easily succeeded in prostrating her at his feet.

" Bend down, " said he severely, as he saw that the Princess still held her head erect.

A tremor passed through her frame, but she bowed her head, not being able to divine what penance would be imposed upon her. The Abbot allowed her to guess at it, by the way in which he still pressed upon her proud shoulders, as with all his might and main he inclined the upper part of her body towards the legs of the armchair, but she could not escape the threatened punishment, or perhaps she had not sufficient power of will to do so.

Thurzo the Abbot, having seized three small, thorny, and supple twigs, began to strike vigorously upon the two vast disks that the Princess, in her awkward posture, presented to the priest. Hurried, but firm strokes fell upon her crupper, of which the luminous silk of the tight and narrow skirt did not suffice to hide the curves, but even revealed the secret valley, which by its dark shade divided this brilliant moon into two equal parts. As she felt the smart of the first cuts, the Princess tried to rise.

" Oh no ! Not that, not that !" she exclaimed in a real rage. " Let me go ! This I cannot allow ! "

Nevertheless she received the swishing strokes the Abbot counted out for her, about a dozen, that the slight protection of her dress did not prevent her from feeling. Finally, finding herself no longer held down, she rose up again, dishevelled, tears in her eyes, her skirts crumpled, and her mouth dry and feverish.

" What an indignity ! " she murmured, and fled rapidly, while the Abbot did not even deign to leave his armchair.

Adelgonda was waiting for her in the great hall.

" Well, what happened ? "

Elizabeth replied not a word, and shut herself up in her apartments, which astonished Adelgonda, and then caused her to smile. The Princess often passed her nights with her cousin and Ursula, pretexting that not being alone she was less frightened of the numerous ghosts of Seebenstein. But it was rumoured that when the three women were together they slept but little. They were very fatigued upon awaking; the bed next morning looked as if it had been occupied by a horde of barbarians; and it was said that muttered sounds as of kisses had been heard in the darkness.

This time Elizabeth threw herself face downwards on her bed, and hiding her head in the pillows, as if she feared all light and sound, gave free vent to her grief. The acute burning pains which she felt all over her big posteriors were as nothing compared to the shame that had been forced upon her. A miserable

unknown priest had dared to whip her, upon
whom neither her father, severe though he was,
nor her girl lovers, ofttimes jealous, had ever
ventured to lay a finger ; she had been fusti-
gated—the high-born dame ; the rich and pow-
erful Princess. But she had allowed it. What
had come to her pride and will ? Of course she
understood that a priest is God's deputy, and
that a whipping inflicted by him is not the same
thing as ordinary violence. But no matter, a
Princess of her rank and station should not put
up with such penances, even at the hands of
her confessor.

First, she thought of sending him away, but
she had had such trouble to find a chaplain.
Besides, might he not go and tell all over
Vienna, in the houses where he visited, how he
had treated proud Princess Bathory ? She
would become the laughing-stock of all the
aristocracy. The best thing to be done was

to keep him, and to send him to Coventry for a little while, humiliating him, and teazing him in a thousand little pin-pricking ways as a punishment. To all appearances he would put up with all this, and would become more gentle. Being poor, he doubtless desired to keep on receiving the ample salary she doled out to him. And what a bad effect it would have for him if he left a castle almost as soon as he had entered it. This last thought nursed her to sleep, after having uttered a cry of fury when dropping her petticoat, she was obliged to note that the freshly-gathered twigs had left greenish traces on her dress behind.

" This shall cost him dear ! " she inwardly exclaimed.

The next morning at mass, the chaplain was alone with his respondent. The Princess had forbidden all her domestics to assist, but the Abbot did not appear to notice that the chapel was empty. At meal-times, the Princess talked a great deal, but without once addressing a word to Thurzo. When he spoke, no one replied. While serving the repasts, domestics spilt wine or sauce on his clothes, as if by accident. His face lost none of its placidity.

These hostile and aggressive ways lasted one whole week. At the end of that time, the priest summoned Ursula, and she continued to salute him with respect, despite the Princess's prohibition. He told her that he wished to see her mistress.

" Her Highness is not in her room, " said Ursula.

" Has she gone out ? "

" No, " replied Ursula. " She is doubtless in the privy. "

Ursula could not refrain from smiling at the idea that such a proud Princess should be a slave to these vulgar needs.

" Well then, " said the Abbot, quite seriously, " go and fetch her. I would speak with her without further delay. "

Ursula laughed no longer. What a fearful command for her to have to execute ! Nevertheless she went to the privy, which was situated in the castle courtyard, and knocked at the door, saying timidly :

" My lord Abbot desires to see your Highness at once. "

" What mean you by ' at once ' ? "

" Verily, he said he would not wait. "

" Great heaven ! "

Although the Princess poked fun at the priest, she was greatly agitated when he gave an order, even if it was only Ursula repeating it.

" Princess, " said the priest, appearing in the middle of the courtyard, and speaking in front of all the servants, " I await you in my apartment. "

She followed him at once. Vainly did she jeer at him when he was absent, it sufficed that she heard his grave and authoritative voice to feel her pride subjugated.

As soon as they were in the apartments, the Abbot closed the door, and said in a tone of irritation, but without lifting his voice :

" Will you please tell me, madam, why you caused me to come to your castle ? "

" To be my chaplain—you know that very well. "

It was with a mutinous tendency that she laid stress upon the " my " which showed what she thought of her power on her estate.

" A chaplain is not a buffoon, " he replied. " It is not the man you have insulted, but God Himself. "

" Pardon ! " said she, beginning to tremble.

" You wished to be revenged on me for having chastised you. You tried to punish me.

But try first to punish yourself for your own sensuality. "

" My lord Abbot ! " she cried imploringly, " I beg you to grant me your pardon. I am full of repentance, I assure you. "

" You do not repent at all, " he replied, " but you are afraid—ay, afraid of the penance you deserve, and which I am about to inflict upon you. "

" I crave your clemency ! " she exclaimed.

" Ask your own self for pity. Each of your errors brings its own repression. For the last eight days, you have humiliated and over-whelmed with ignominy a servant of Jesus—a priest ! All this matters little as far as the man is concerned, but out of respect for the vest-ments I wear, I cannot suffer such an insult to pass. Therefore I command that you serve me to-night at dinner. "

" Oh, my lord Abbot ! "

" You will wait upon me, or I leave the castle. "

" At any rate, " she said, " let there be none but us in the dining-hall. "

" Your cousins and the serving maids shall be present.   In their presence did you humiliate a priest.   Now shall you honour him before their eyes. "

She had been in fear of a worse penance, and was almost pleased that the Abbot had spared it her, but she thought herself free too soon.

" Now kneel before me, for the other penance, " said Thurzo.

This was a cruel surprise for her. She grew pale and shuddered.

" Oh ! my lord Abbot, tell me that it will not be like the first time ? " she asked, her eyes dilated with anguish.

" It will be a little more severe. "

" Oh, my God ! " she exclaimed, and was

about to kneel, resigned and mastered, when he said to her :

" But beforehand, take off your skirt ! "

" That I will not do ! You will never force me to that ! " and she seemed as if breaking out into open revolt.

The priest's eyes sparkled.

" Shall I do it for you ? "

" Dare to do so ! " she replied, her fists clenched, her head thrown back, her lithe body erect and straining, in readiness to defend herself.

" Your servants shall help me, if I cannot get the better of you alone, sacrilegious woman ! "

The word " sacrilege " shattered at once all Elizabeth's ideas of resistance.

" My father, " said she submissively, " I will do whatever you want of me, but I conjure you, do not force me to disrobe before you at this moment. "

" Why do you not wish to undress now ? "

" Because—because I am not—not in a fit state to show myself to you. "

" Are you uneasy about me or yourself ? " he asked. " Methinks it is more coquetry that troubles you than pudicity. Perchance wish you to seduce me ? But if your flesh should not appear to-day in its usual brilliancy, or accompanied by its customary perfume, will not that be quite natural and in keeping, since it is unveiled merely to do penance, and to lower proud feelings all the better ? "

She did not resist, for she was broken in spirit, crushed beneath the burden of shame. She unfastened her skirt and petticoat herself, but with what awkward slowness ! Meanwhile a bitter scent hovered about her more and more, reminding the priest, not of voluptuous feminine furbelows, but of the secret spot where the Princess had been seated a few moments before.

" Off with your drawers now ! " was the next order of the confessor.

She looked up with an imploring glance, but the Abbot was in no humour to pardon.

Naked, save her chemise and stockings, she fell across the priest's armchair, hiding herself as much as possible, in the dishevelled tresses of her luxuriant hair. Suddenly, he lifted her filmy last garment, of soft silk, and remained as if dazzled at the sight of the divided fleshly circle, so solid, vast ; the fair skin tightly stretched over its surface, and so beautifully rotund. The sepia-like hue that threw its shade over the deepest recesses of her body, and the strong odour that arose therefrom, far from being repugnant, seemed to delight him, as if it reminded him of the rind and perfume of some favourite fruit. He experienced such a craving to press and embrace these superb buttocks, that he could not refrain from opening the slightly sullied cheeks, and even went so far as to slide his finger to the verge of the impure orifice. She shuddered, and half turned her head. Thurzo, to prevent her suspecting anything, was obliged to seize the birch hurriedly, and risking to draw blood, strike pitilessly on the spot which was so delicate and which he was tempted to caress. Astounded at such an unexpected and brutal blow, she gave a start of pain, uttered a shriek, and her eyes filled with tears.

" Oh, not there ! For pity's sake ! 'Tis odious ! "

The priest then began to swish at her big buttocks, but now and again, much more gently than the first time, he returned to the dark valley, seemingly amusing himself by searching there with the ends of the sharp twigs, and probably pleased at the bounds and starts, writhings and wrigglings of his victim. Now

and again, convulsive movements of agony
caused the lovely mountain of flesh to upheave,
and all sombre shadows faded away. The two
cheeks now only formed an enormous broad
bottom, red all over. In the place of the shady
streak, the purple eyelet hole was stretched to
bursting, as if ready to give some salute of
mocking indecency. But the Abbot hardly
had time to contemplate the sudden transformation, when the reddish-mauve aperture
disappeared; the valley grew deep again, the
magnificent bottom was once more divided
into two equal parts, and the priest, furious,
one might have thought, at such a sudden
change, began to birch her more vigorously
than ever.

Drops of blood, like heavy rubies, trickled
down the thighs, falling in a carmine shower
from the fiery moon, whose bruises, and red,
pink, and violet marks were enhanced more

strangely by the milky fairness of the other parts of the Princess's body.

" I pardon you ! " at last said the cruel chaplain, throwing down the birch-rod.

She rose, shaken from head to foot by long and heavy sobs, and getting into her drawers, petticoat, and dress, went out of the Abbot's quarters.

" Will you come for a ride on horseback ? " asked Adelgonda, as the Princess went back to her own apartments.

" Yes, " she answered, " by and by. "

Half an hour afterwards, she reappeared, not wishing that anyone should guess she had been punished. It would have been difficult to detect how she had suffered and wept, while the priest, at his window, could see his penitent victim riding her prancing steed, between Adelgonda and Lenchen. Her vast posteriors, encased in an emerald-green riding habit, spread themselves over her saddle with such reposeful majesty, that it was impossible to guess that a painful birching onslaught had just bruised them all over. But the effort she was obliged to make to hide her pain, exhausted all her energy. When she came home, she went to bed, and did not appear at dinner. Thus she did not have to wait upon the Abbot in public.

From that day forth, when the priest was present, she showed herself so gentle with her maids, Adelgonda, and Lenchen, that they were astounded. She also attended mass with exemplary assiduity, and frequented the chapel regularly. She confessed weekly, and Thurzo remarked that she never made any avowals of violence, fury, cruelty, or pride. She only accused herself of being a prey to the obsession of lust, from which she could not escape. What was strange, was that every two or three nights, she shut herself up in her apartments with Adelgonda, Lenchen, and Ursula, when, despite the thickness of the walls and the hangings masking every door, a noise was heard that the servants called the song of the witches' sabbath. It was a weird chorus formed of groans, moans, cries of pleasure and tortured shrieks; with now and again the tumult of a combat, as if a struggling woman became finally mastered.

One day, a pantry-maid praised the Princess's beneficent kindness as shown to her, remarking how her mistress had changed for the better of late, but a comrade—lady's maid to Elizabeth Bathory—shrugged her shoulders, as she said :

" She restrains herself before the Abbot because she is frightened of him, but as soon as his back is turned, she makes us pay dearly for her forbearance. If you had been to the

privy with Ursula, as I did, you would have
seen the poor girl's backside. Soon, she will
not be able to sit down at all. Do I not speak
the truth, Ursula ? "

That poor serving wench bent her head and
blushed without vouchsafing a reply.

" Then there is poor little Lenchen ! She
receives more cuts daily than a grenadier could
support. "

The plain truth of the matter was that the
penances of the Abbot Thurzo, instead of
softening the Princess's pride, served only to
cause it to rise up in revolt. Now she was full
of cruelty, which refused to be satiated. It
appeared to her that by dint of shame and tortures inflicted upon others, she would forget
those that had been imposed upon her, and so
reconquer the feeling of power she had lost.

Her cruelties had another kind of reason
and the Abbot was destined soon to discover

what that was. One day, a timid knock was heard at his door. He came and opened it. Then he caught sight of Lenchen, out of breath, her hair in disorder, her short skirts all crumpled. The chaplain also noticed that her eyes were red, and her cheeks scarlet and shining, as if she had wept much.

" I am very unhappy, " she said to the Abbot, who was rather surprised at seeing her, " and as nobody here will listen to me, Ursula being as wretched as I am, I have come to you. You, perchance, may take pity on me ! "

" I feel compassion towards all suffering, my dear little Lenchen, " rejoined the priest, " and you particularly inspire me with too much sympathy not to make me try to relieve you in your misfortune as far as it is possible for me to do. Sit there, near me, and tell me what brings you to my side. "

" This is what it is, " said she. " I really think she wants to kill me. "

" Kill you? But who could desire your death, my dear child? "

" Elizabeth! "

" What!—the Princess, your cousin? "

" She is not my cousin, " Lenchen went on; " only my half-sister. My father had me with a servant-maid of the castle who died bringing me into the world. He loved me very much, and in his will that Ursula has seen, he bequeathed me part of his fortune. Elizabeth has always hidden this document from me, having perhaps destroyed or made away with it; besides, she has never spoken to me of our real relationship. For everybody, I am but her cousin. She would be pleased if some misfortune should befall me. Most likely she will not wait till then. She is quite capable of murdering me, even as she massacred your predecessor, the poor old chaplain. She used to beat him with her saddle-girths. He lost his life under her blows in this very room. See, there, where you may view the trace of blood-stains. The martyr fell against the wall, where the imprint of his hand still remains, and he was quickly buried and by stealth. Know you why she murdered him? Simply because my father on his deathbed asked to see me before he expired, having moreover charged the unfortunate priest to reveal to me the secret of my birth. I learnt all this later from Ursula, who is cognizant of things that my sister thinks she alone knows. What Elizabeth would like is that I should die of grief brought on by ill-treatment. Fancy! she would come into all my fortune. Besides—but this is extraordinary—she is jealous of me."

"Jealous of you?"

"Yes, yes! She says that I am pretty—

oh ! not to me, but she has told other people so, and when I am talked about, when anyone looks at me, she flies out in fearful fits of temper. She wishes she was the only pretty woman in the world, and thus hating me, she tortures me every day. Not a week passes but what I am whipped. Yet I am over fifteen. I am no longer a little girl ! I don't think I am very wicked. This morning, I fell down, while strolling, and dirtied my dress a little. She threw herself madly upon me, boxed my ears, and as I answered her, she struck me again, and tried to beat me with a handful of twigs. But you may guess that I defended myself. So then she called Adelgonda, and both together they whipped me until the blood came. Look and see that I tell no lies ! "

Poor little Lenchen's petticoats had been so often lifted, and she had been taught so few lessons of chastity, that she uncovered her

darling, tiny bum quite naturally, and without
the least shamefaced hesitation. Truly, however, a priest is somewhat like a doctor, and
all lascivious ideas awakened by the sight of
these lovely charms were bound to fade away
and be forgotten beneath Lenchen's numerous
scars, and the bleeding wound that could be
seen where the fleshy half-moons were divided.
But what caused the Abbot to marvel was that
from the loins to the thighs there was not a
spot unmarked with what looked liked a
pattern of tiny, round knobs in bold relief.
He asked her the meaning of this.

" The reason is, " she said, " because Elizabeth beats me with a woden spade pierced
with little round holes, which she also
uses for Ursula and the other wenches,
and each time this colander-like instrument
of torture comes down on one's skin it
brings up big blisters. My sister always

says to me and the other girls she strikes in the same way : ' You won't be inclined now to show your backsides to the men, you nasty, dirty sows ! ' She pretends she is punishing us for an alleged indecent act we were supposed to have committed during the summer. I had been out bathing with Ursula and the other girls. When we wished to leave the water, we were a little time before we could find our clothes, and some roguish lads accidentally passing by, amused themselves by looking at us from a distance. No doubt we were guilty of imprudence, but is that such a crime, and does not Elizabeth do much worse when she gives her orders to her steward or coachman while she is stark naked at her toilet ? "

The Abbot promised Lenchen to persuade the Princess not to beat her any more, and indeed, for a few days, neither Lenchen nor Ursula had to complain of being misused.

Then the Princess ceased all restraint over herself, and began once more to whip her sister and her maid.

It may be asked why the Abbot Thurzo remained in the house of a woman who seemed to fear him, but who never ceased declaring to all about her that she detested him. Did he hope to convert her? She had no sooner left the confessional, or the altar steps, than she could be seen giving way with the greatest freedom to her passions of lechery and violence. Her superstitious devotion, far from excusing her vices, was more of an insult to religion, the sacred character of which she compromised by her assiduity as far as pious practices were concerned, mingled with her steadfast attachment to the most odious sensual passions.

* * *

Towards the end of September, shortly

before leaving Seebenstein to return to Vienna, the Princess gave a grand party to which she invited the noble families of the surrounding districts. These festivals of Seebenstein were original and peculiar inasmuch as no men were ever invited. Women, or young girls, danced with each other. Their mothers, out of sheer simplicity, or having but an imperfect knowledge of their hostess's habits, found this sexless ball much more respectable and decent than ordinary dancing assemblies.

The dances in the drawing-rooms were accompanied by a rustic ball in the courtyard for the servants and the peasants. There could men be seen, as the Princess was unable to do without a coachman, butler, head cook and other male domestics, but her ladies' maids were expressly forbidden to dance, or even to show themselves there. All four of them had to remain in the vestibule leading to her apartments.

A vast crowd of guests had arrived in the reception rooms. There could be seen luxurious tresses drawn up to show white napes of necks sparkling with diamonds ; or heavy, long, fair or chestnut curls floating as far as the loins ; gauzy muslin dresses, or silken robes forming stiff, unwilling, rich folds. In the midst of the yard, lit up by lanterns, were white woollen skirts, silk aprons embroidered in yellow and red, and the hair was tied up with handkerchiefs of a thousand multicoloured designs.

The Princess danced but little, and it seemed as if her thoughts were far away. The year before, she had been seen to throw herself upon a young girl who pleased her, tearing her away from her mother and sisters, waltzing, and turning giddily with her all the evening. As if by accident, she had coaxed her with rapid, cunning caresses, which seemed singular by dint of repetition : fingers slipping far below the waist; hands surtively sliding between the thighs ; breasts panting and rubbing against a childish bosom—finally, incapable of controlling her desire, she had dragged the innocent girl to her own bed, where she had little trouble in putting all resistance to sleep, and forcing her to endure her weird whims.

But this time she seemed indifferent to the dancing lasses, and her mind was full of grave cares. She left the ball every moment, going and glancing in the vestibule, where the maids were. Once or twice she went down into the courtyard, looking all about her, as she passed in the midst of the village merry-go-rounds. At last, she went upstairs, as far as the apartments of the Abbot Thurzo, flattened her ear against his door, and then, returning to her serving-maids, she told one of them to go at once and fetch the chaplain.

When the priest appeared, she did not rise from the armchair where she was seated, and imitated, in a way, the priest's own attitude when she had been to visit him.

" Aha ! my lord Abbot, there you are at last ! " she exclaimed in mad, passionate rage. " Do you think I have engaged you here in my castle to debauch my serving wenches ? Oh ! do not feign such surprise. I know that Ursula is in your room, and this is not the first time she has gone there. "

" Did I debauch you, during the two visits you made me ? " replied the Abbot smiling.

The Princess grew scarlet with passion.

" I will not have my maids visiting you. If they want advice, or need to make the avowal of some sin, let them kneel in the confessional. Moreover, in future, they shall ask their rule of conduct of another confessor. Ah ! ah ! " she continued, noticing that the priest had started, " you did not think I should send you packing so soon, my lord Abbot ? "

" I had made up my mind to go, " he replied. " After what Ursula told me. "

" Soho ! You have gained her confidence, and you have secrets together. You have not lost your time, that I paid for. Since when is she your mistress ? "

" She came not to me as a seductress, but as an unfortunate woman, complaining and asking for pity. "

" You do well to tell of that. She will not be seated on a bed of roses this night, and will not sleep with her door open. I will teach her to go and complain of her mistress. A careful flogging and a locked cell—that is what awaits her. "

" It is you who are about to be chastised, " he said, " and at once, for your cruelties and your crimes. "

So saying, he seized her violently by the hair.

She had no time to manifest her astonishment or to try any kind of resistance. Her magnificent fair locks came unbound, and rolled instantly away from her brow, becoming a chain, a torturing impediment, instead of the admirable ornament they had just been. Her buttocks, which had seemed glued to the cushions of the armchair, were forced away, torn from the seat; and the Princess, bent down, blinded by the heavy thick tufts of hair that covered her eyes; her neck wounded by two jewelled pins which, having been disarranged, stuck in her flesh, was forced to follow her tormentor where it pleased him to lead her. In this way the Abbot conducted her into her own bedchamber, and suddenly letting go the chain of hair by which he held her, the Princess fell face downwards on her bed. He did not allow her time enough to rise, but mounting on the couch himself, he rode this mutinous mare a-straddle, his face towards her feet, pressing her roughly between his knees, and pressing now and again on her shoulders with a bound, into which he threw all his weight. Bending over her enormous dome, luminous beneath her silken ball-dress, he deftly pulled up all that veiled it : petticoats, skirts, and light chemise. He pulled open, and pushed down to the ancles her small drawers. Her twin mountains of flesh appeared so close one to the other that their shadowy valley was hardly to be seen. The Abbot leant over as if to inhale the aroma rising therefrom.

" Good ! " said he. " Your backside is perfumed to-day. You doubtless expected my caress, or perhaps some other far less brutal. "

The Princess did not reply, but clenched her

teeth, and closed her fists in impotent rage.

At last the Abbot, who was looking about for some weapon with which to strike this haughty crupper, suddenly perceived on a small table within his reach, the spade of agony, its holes sticky with congealed blood, which served to torture Lenchen and Ursula. When the Princess felt the first blows of this fearful instrument, she shivered, bounded, and writhed to such an extent that the Abbot fancied for a moment his wicked mount was about to throw him off her back. Nevertheless, he was able to hold her and strike her at his ease. She then set about groaning and shrieking in such wise that she was heard as far as the ball-room, which however was far enough away. Adelgonda and a few friends recognising Elizabeth's voice, grew uneasy, and rushed out together with thes erving lasses who had remained in the vestibule. As they opened the door, they saw the vast and massive backside, all bare, crimsoned already and studded with blisters, framed round with the priest's black robe, and surmounted by his bust. The Abbot flourished the instrument that the Princess called with barbarous irony, " the draughtsman, " and it could be seen that for a man unused to wielding such a weapon, he managed to handle it pretty well.

" What is the matter ? What are you about ? " exclaimed all the women.

" I am correcting the Princess," the Abbot simply replied, without changing his posture, or interrupting his shower of chastising blows. " She would, I fancy, be grateful to you, if you would kindly withdraw. I never thought of inflicting a public penance upon her. "

Adelgonda knew what narrow frontiers lay between cruelty and pleasure ; and she did not think for a moment that Thurzo was really punishing the Princess. So she was more amused than frightened at the sight. But the other young girls appeared to be suffocating with fear and shame at the view of this flagellating penance which was so shameless and humiliating that they thought an abominable sin must have given rise to it. As for the serving maids they were right joyous to see their mistress thus treated. Few of the women, notwithstanding, hurried to leave the bedchamber. To get them to go, the Abbot was obliged to turn round a little, bend his head down towards the Princess and apprise her that her shrieks had drawn quite a large audience.

" Is it your wish that these ladies should remain to hear you ? " he asked, " or would you prefer that they should go away ? "

" Let them be gone ! Let them go ! " she repeated, in the midst of her moaning, her voice half smothered by her hair and the skirts of the Abbot's gown that covered her face.

At a sign from the chaplain they went away whispering. They had hardly departed, when Thurzo, judging that the guilty bottom had been seared enough, slipped off the bed, and threw the spade out of window. He was still standing in the recess of the casement, when the Princess, who was quickly on her feet, struck him in the face.

" Ah ! " she cried, " as God's my witness I have suffered everything at your hands, but this last odious outrage—ah ! no ! no ! I'll not put up with it ! "

" Be quiet, " said the Abbot, holding her fast, powerless to do harm, " be assured that I never had any idea of chastising you before your servants, for I do not pretend to destroy your authority over them. Your shrieks alone brought them hither. "

" And why did you inflict your frightful

penance in the very middle of the ball ? "

" Your crimes revolted me; and so did all those I have just been told about. The girls who informed me were right to do so. Above all, was I alarmed at those you are planning against defenceless young females. This time I struck you in a rage, with no consideration. The flagellation, however rigorous it may have seemed to you, is notwithstanding out of all proportion to the quantity of iniquitous acts you have committed. For you deserve no childish slapping, and God reserves for you no secret penance, Elizabeth Bathory, but death in public, on the red scaffold, if you continue to lead the same execrable existence. The murder had but one witness whose troublesome revelations you have been able to stifle up to the present, but the assassinations of Lenchen and Ursula will be known to all, of that you may rest assured ! "

The Princess had got quite pale; but she tried to hide her emotion.

" So you believe all these stories? " she said, in a disdainful tone.

" They do not seem to be invented, but painfully real, when one has lived a few days in your house. "

" This is too much! " she cried, and seizing a short dagger that hung against the wall, she rushed upon the priest. The Abbot repulsed her assault, and tore the poniard from her, but he could not prevent the Princess from hanging on to his long black garments, while she scratched his hands and face.

This struggle ended in a strange way. The two combatants drew away from each other, each giving vent to a cry. The Princess held a long beard in her hand : that of the Abbot Thurzo, which had remained in her grasp, and the holy man, now with smooth cheeks, no longer appeared as a venerable priest, but had become a young fellow, with fresh red lips, and palpitating nostrils.

"Martin Frankestein!" she exclaimed, with mingled surprise and fear.

"So why feign any longer?" rejoined the false Abbot, as he threw off his grey wig, and let his natural abundant dark hair be seen.

"Oh! sacrilegious man!" she cried, in horror, "who has dared to put on sacerdotal robes so as to penetrate into my castle, to spy into my life, and discover all the secrets of my body! What shame! How could I have abandoned myself to you, unworthy profaner, filthy libertine? I know not what instinct warned me in spite of all that a good priest would never have treated me with such ignominious grossness. How now can I wipe out this outrage? You have seen me naked! Aha! you shall not leave this place alive, I warrant you.   I'll punish such abominable audacity. "

" I will go forth with my life—and with
you, " was his rejoinder.

" Silence, wretch ! "

" Did you not confess to me, when quite a
young girl, that you loved me ? "

" A mere joke !   I wished to mock at your
fatuity, and your foolish pretentions. "

" I have never been able to forget that
childish troth.   I said to myself that I would
possess you in spite of everything, even were
I forced to violate you ! "

" Monster ! "

" Insult me not, but listen.   For some time
past, I know what you are.   In Vienna, you are
spoken of as being the most vicious, and even
one of the most criminal of all women, whose
great name and fortune alone protected from
the police.   No matter !   Your striking beauty
had bewitched me.   I only saw that, and blind

to all the rest, I said to myself that with my
energy and will, I would convert you in course
of time, cure you of your cruel lusts, and make
of you a good, gentle, and loving woman, as
nature has decreed. In all your wicked personality there was one side accessible to goodness. You were pious, or rather superstitious,
but a clever man could profit by these religious
inclinations to drag your vices out of you by
sheer force, and drive away the infamous demon
who had taken possession of your soul. Thus
did I try the experiment. Hearing that you
were in want of a confessor, I introduced
myself to you. I was able to disguise myself
artfully enough and play my part sufficiently
well to nourish the hope of remaining by your
side. You cannot believe what singular and
varied emotions crowded into my brain when
forced to inflict a penance. For me it was
needful expiation. "

" Oh ! infamy ! What horror ! "

" Ay, I felt certain that your pride required to be lowered, by applying to you, at the age of eighteen, the humiliating punishments that your father, too weak and good, had spared you. It seemed to me that little by little you would lose your superb haughtiness ; becoming better, more gentle and humble, and this hope as well as the pleasure of contemplating your gracefulness and your unknown charms and beauties, gave me courage to strike you. But how much would I have preferred to have showered kisses upon you instead of blows ! "

" Prithee cease these untimely declarations," said the Princess, turning away her glance. " They only increase the disgust and hatred with which you inspire me. Believe me when I say that what I suffered at the hands of a priest, because he represents God on this earth, I would endure from no man, father, king, or emperor ! "

" Not even from a husband ? "

" I shall never have one ! Men are too deeply repugnant to me ! "

Frankestein gazed at the Princess with sparkling eyes, in which was revealed the flame of fierce will.

" You must be mine, " said he, " and at once ! "

She shrugged her shoulders contemptuously, but almost at the same time she uttered a howl of pain. He had seized her hands and squeezed them with such force that he made the bones crack. He bent her down in his vigorous grip, causing her to kneel at his feet.

" Oh, you coward ! " she said again and again, choking, furious, and becoming more incapable of resistance every moment that her rage robbed her of all energy.

He kept her in this posture for some time. When she had no more courage, broken down by fatigue, and had not got the least thought of resistance left, he threw her backwards on the carpet, and brutally tearing her legs wide apart, penetrated into her beautiful body. His kisses and conjunction caused a few thrills to run through her frame, and then she remained impassible.

" You will no longer jeer at me, " said he, with a triumphant smile, " for you cannot disown me now ! "

She remained still, her eyes closed, as if fainting. Her face, with its severe features and imperious mouth, was suddenly softened. By reason of the deep embrace, the woman seemed to have become a child again, and Frankestein, standing in front of her, joyfully contemplated this lucky transformation.

Elizabeth however, opened her eyes. She

looked down, and saw her petticoat and chemise still thrown back, exposing her naked
belly, and on her thigh trembled a drop of
blood, like a crimson pearl. Her eyes blazed;
all her innate passionate fury returned to her,
and at once she sprang to her feet. She
clutched the dagger which Frankestein had
thrown aside on the table.

"Die, profane wretch!" she cried, as she
stabbed him with all her strength.

The blow was well aimed, and Frankestein,
his heart profoundly pierced, fell without a
word.

Elizabeth, drunk with vengeance, leant over
her victim, her heart leaping in her full breast,
and radiantly joyful, she followed to the end
all the convulsions of death.

When the man moved no more, she heaved
a sigh, and seemed delivered of some immense
burden. But her joy did not last long. As

she dropped her skirts, her fingers were
bedewed with blood, in which mingled some
other mysterious velvety liquid. Her arms
stiffened and stretched themselves out ; her
contracted lineaments expressed frightful repul-
sion, as her whole body was throbbing with
horror and disgust. She rushed to Frankestein's corpse, tore the bloody dagger from
his wound, and struck her own deathblow
with it.

* *

Thus, like some virtuous Lucretia, died this
criminal Princess, as proud of her virginity, as
she was avidious of all lechery, and who
wished to curb each and every one beneath the
yoke of her beauty without abandoning herself
to any.

In the very night of the rejoicings, Ursula

discovered the two corpses. After the first moment of stupor and affright had passed over, the news caused a feeling of happiness and relief to most of the guests, for the Princess was more hated than loved.

A few days later, Prince Bathory's will was found. In it he acknowledged Lenchen as his daughter, and bequeathed all his fortune to her, in case Elizabeth should die before her. The young girl needed no such splendid inheritance to console her for the loss of her sister. The day after the funeral, when the new mistress of Seebenstein received the vassals of her domains, seated in the high oaken armchair of the Bathory Princess, it was remarked that from time to time she could not refrain from rubbing her posteriors, and that, graceful and pretty though she might be, her bearing was far being as solemn as the occasion demanded.

This caused one of the servants to remark :
" She does not weep, but her bottom mourns
for her ! It is easy to see that her sister's
generosity has left more than one remembrance
on her plump backside ! "

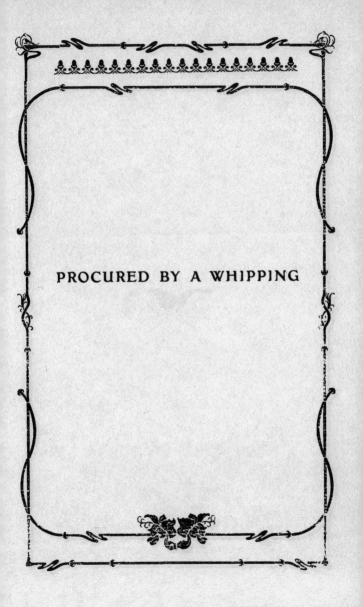

PROCURED BY A WHIPPING

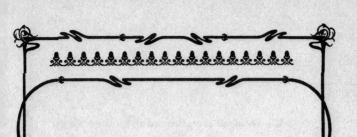

PROCURED BY A WHIPPING

A few years ago, I was summoned to Le Perreux, in the environs of Paris, by a rich retired tradesman, who had asked me to paint his portrait. I belong to the school of the great artist, La Tour, who delighted in long and patient studious work, and I did not conceal from my client that two or three sittings would not be enough for me to terminate a good, finished sketch, as he had thought at first.

" Take your own time, " said he, " I am entirely at your disposal. "

We arranged the price and about the sittings.
He was to stand before my easel every morning
at nine o'clock, but as he was in a hurry to
have his picture, and fearing that if I went
backwards and forwards to Paris, I might miss
a day, or be late, he begged me earnestly to
remain down at Le Perreux until his portrait
should be finished. He even offered to put
me up in a charming little pavilion at the bottom
of his garden. This building had an exit
leading into a small alley, and I could thus
live from each afternoon until the next morning
in my own house, so to speak, and quite at
liberty.

I accepted his offer, although it seemed to
me a little hard to pass several weeks at Le
Perreux. But my mistress was away from
Paris ; my afternoons were free, and this
portrait, which was to be generously paid, was
an interesting piece of work. My host had a

most uncommon face, energetic and ferocious, the physiognomy of an audacious brigand, and I was all agog to fix its strange character on my canvas.

After the first sitting, and the exquisite little luncheon that followed, I returned to my building feeling slightly tired, for the commencement of my work is always something of a painful strain for me.

I inspected the first floor, which was destined for me, with its vast rooms, charmingly upholstered and fitted with pretty furniture, pleased to find a comfortable sofa; when through my open windows, floated a little girl's voice which drew my attention at once.

The casement gave on to a tiny garden belonging to a little house; climbing plants and the capricious foliage of wild vines formed a sweet and light screen, serving as a shutter, through which I could see all that was going on at my neighbour's, without it being possible to suspect that I was playing the spy.

There is something alluring for me about children, especially little girls, because their features are as yet undecided as to contours and character. Everything is left to the imagination of the beholder ; and the brightness of their skin and childish, artless grace is all very engaging. We love them for their precocious promise of future beauty, and adore these wee women for the charms and adventures they seem to foreshadow. What fools are severe preachers, and anserous herds, who will not allow that a man should feel ideal, sensual rapture at the sight of a child, considering any caress savouring of sensuality bestowed on a growing lassie, or youth, as a rape and outrage ! I venerate what is as yet undeveloped, the secret flower scarce showing on its stem. It would be absurd to try and pluck it before it had arrived at maturity ; but surely I may feast my eyes on the unopened bud ? I know no more delicious and enticing pastime than to frolic with these pretty dolls. There are caresses, and punishments, in harmony with their years, which bring smiles and tears to fresh young faces, making them contract or brighten, half revealing to me the little woman hidden in the sprightly maid in her teens. Certain drawings of great masters impress me in the same manner. When we study them, we may divine the masterpiece, executed later, but which maybe pleases us more in the simple lines of the rough sketch often still vague, and startling one through the very lack of artifice, like nature herself.

Certainly there was nothing angelic about the little girl I listened to. She was between ten and eleven, plump, with a round, babyish, rosy face ; fair hair falling like a young filly's untrimmed mane on her shoulders, coquettishly tied with a knot of purple ribbon at the neck, but her face was lit up by brilliant, malicious, voluptuous eyes, which were really those of a woman.

Near her a servant girl was sewing. As she was just underneath my window, I got a glimpse of her large, shapely backside, covered by a black skirt, and of which I could see all the curves, by the tension of her body bending over her work. Her short locks of woolly, whitey-brown hair, allowing her fat and short neck to appear between the little curls of the nape and the white, high collar, next attracted my attention, together with her broad shoulders, the elegant little cap, as immaculate as the starched band under her chin, and a corner of her apron hemmed round with cheap imitation lace.

The little girl twisted herself about, writhing,

stretching out her arms, shuffling in the gravel, as if not knowing where to put herself and what to do, as she even scratched her bottom, while the nurse never missed a stitch, chattering away for dear life all the time.

" You may say what you like, Jennie," she said, " your mother is a nasty thing. How she can treat people as she does, I can't make out ! Ah ! if your papa wasn't here, I should have given notice long ago. "

" My poor Rosalie, you needn't tell me you're chummy with pa, that's easily seen. But I can't abear him. "

" Because he gives you many a fine thrashing. But you don't deserve them. Oh no, not at all, neither ! "

Jennie seemed rather worried at being reminded in such an inopportune manner of certain moments of her young life which she doubtless had not had time to forget, judging from the reiterated rubbings with which she kept on gratifying the hinder part of her anatomy.

" Ma licks me just the same, " she rejoined, " but I don't care. I don't bear her any malice. "

" Your ma just pulls up your clothes in fun ; but as for papa, if he corrects you, it's in earnest—to punish you. "

" No, it's 'cos he's wicked. I'm sick of his snout. His face disgusts me. "

" Indeed ? Well, I'll just tell this evening what you said about him. "

" No, no, good little Rosalie, don't, I beg you ! " supplicated Jennie, joining her hands as if in prayer.

The maid did not answer, so Jennie stamped her feet in a rage.

" I'll tell tales too. I'll tell ma that he kissed you, yesterday, on the neck ; and pinched your bum, at lunch, and—"

Rosalie, furious, stuck her needle in the bosom of her dress, and dragging little Jennie towards her by the arm, she shook her roughly several times and threatened her with uplifted hand.

" Just repeat what you said. Go on, say it again ! You don't dare to. That's lucky for you ! Well now, just listen to what I'm going to say. If you go sneaking to your ma and say the least little thing about me, I'll pull down your drawers and with the martinet— you know the one your pa bought—I'll give you a whipping on your bare backside that'll stop you sitting down for a month. Who ever heard of such a nasty little tell-tale ? "

" But you're the sneak ! You tell pa all I do ! "

" Begging your pardon, miss, I try to screen you as much as I can. Besides, your papa ought to know if you've behaved yourself or not. "

" Why he behaves badly to ma ! The other
day, our lady visitors all said so. I heard them
myself ! "

" Your ladies, indeed ! They're all bitches,
and so is your ma ! Only think that the night
your father went up to Paris, missus comes to
my room in her chemise, and wakes me up.
' Rosalie, ' says she, ' I'm so frightened, all
alone in my bed. Come and sleep with me. '
' Yes, madame, ' says I, rubbing my eyes. It
amused me as much as going to be hung. So
I changes my linen, follows her, and gets between the sheets with her. First of all, she
starts jawing like the deuce. Clatter, clatter ;
cackle, cackle ! I shuts my eyes, just answering ' yes' and ' no' or nothing at all. But
she keeps on chattering. I loses patience.
' For goodness sake, madame, ' says I, ' let
me go to sleep, if you wants your work done
to-morrow ! ' She says not another word, and

blows out the candle. I turns my backside to her, thinking she'd finished her gossip. But no, the real fun hadn't yet begun! She starts caressing me, and although I shakes her off quite rude, and puffed and blowed to show her she was teazing me, she still kept on with her larks. She pinched my bum, stuck her finger in my dirty bottom-hole, so that I almost felt inclined, saving your reverence, to let go the painter, just to give her a lesson in decent behaviour and teach her manners. At last—only fancy!—she slips her hand between my legs. That was quite enough for me! I gives her a first-class kick in the shins. 'What's the matter with you, Rosalie?' says she, in surprise. 'Madame, I'm a honest girl. I ain't a-going to let myself be touched like that!'
'I touch you? You're mad or dreaming.'
'I ain't dreaming, and I know what I say. Let me be, or I'm off back to my bed, and I

swear to you that to-morrow I'll kick up a shindy before master and everybody. ' So finally she let me alone, and I was able to go to sleep. But you may say what you like, missus is a real dirty beast ! "

" What harm was there in all that ? " said little Jennie, with widely-opened, astonished eyes. " Ma only wanted to tickle you, just for fun. Why did you not let her, if that would amuse her ? You are a stupid. When I play with Hortense, I tickle her; she jumps, and holloas, and wriggles about, laughing fit to die. It's so funny ! Poor ma, she's awfully bored when she's in bed with pa. I often hear her say to him in the morning : ' Go on, get up, you can't do anything ! ' "

" My word ! " replied Rosalie, " he did something when he made you ! It's true you're no great shakes. "

" Rosalie, " said little Jennie, suddenly grow-

ing thoughtful, " explain me what this means.
Papa, when he's in a temper, shouts out to ma
that he ain't my father. "

"'Ah! he says that, does he? Well, perhaps he's right. He ought to know. "

Their amiable chat had reached thus far,
when the sound of a woman's voice issued
from the villa, calling for Rosalie. The servant dropped her work, and the child bent her
steps towards the middle of the garden, where
some gymnastic apparatus was fitted up. She
hung on to the trapeze, drew herself up, stood
on the bar, and swung there for a few minutes.

She moved her body most gracefully, trying to
go quicker and quicker. She would first bend her
legs, crouching down in the midst of her waving
skirts, and then standing erect, she flew backwards and forwards, her frock clinging to her
posteriors. All of a sudden, she sat down,
slipped from the trapeze, and hung by the feet,

head downwards. Her hair swept the gravel path, her petticoats flew over her head, and the two plump, dimpled cheeks of her bottom, of a pinky red from her exercise and exertions, were fully exposed to my sight through the wide slit of her knickers. In this position, she resembled some strange flower; her petticoats looking like the petals, and the miniature hemispheres, the calyx. I was quite engrossed with her graceful posture, when a rather tall, thin man, with a tired face, rheumy eyes, and a red beard, rushed at her. The gymnastic little lady heard his footstep on the pebbles of the path and jumped rapidly away from the trapeze. But she had no time to stand upright. The man was quickly behind her, and kept her on her knees, her petticoats still thrown over her head.

" I'll teach you to show your behind when you're doing gymnastics, " he shouted.

" But it's not my fault, pa! The buttons of my knickers are busted. "

" You ought to have sewn them on again. That's easy enough, but I warrant you won't be able to take off the red pair of drawers I'm going to cut out for you! "

" Oh! Oh! Don't, pa, please! Do forgive me! Oh! Oh! "

The man pulled a leather-thonged martinet out of his overcoat pocket, and gave severe cuts with it on the cheeks of the tiny lass's bottom.

Jennie, on her knees, held in bondage by her petticoats, trapped in her fallen drawers, tried to escape from this rigorous flagellation. She turned about on all-fours, but in vain, all round her tormentor, so that at every step she made beneath my window, I saw either her bum growing redder and more bruised, or her weeping face.

When at last, little drops of blood started on her smarting skin, the child was able to get away, and ran with her clothes still up through the garden. Her cruel corrector, satisfied with his work, did not dream of pursuing her, but was content to look at the girlish body he had just flayed, as he nodded his head menacingly at her, and threw the martinet after her retreating figure. It fell at the child's feet. Jennie turned her face to the garden wall and hiding her features in her hands, whined and sobbed without paying attention to her dress which was still round her head, or her drawers dragging at her heels.

After having strolled round his garden for a few minutes, the father went quickly indoors. When Jennie heard him going up the stone steps leading into the house, she turned and put her tongue out at him.

" I'll have my revenge, see if I don't ! " she muttered between her teeth.

Then, finding under her heel the instrument of torture—the wretched martinet that had just torn her bottom to pieces—the girl looked cautiously all around, and seeing no one, quickly threw the leather ' cat ' over the wall into my host's garden, and with her petticoats still disordered she scampered to the kitchen of her dwelling.

" Rosalie! Rosalie! Come and put me on some cold cream! Make haste! "

" Ah! Pa has given you a whipping, eh? Serves you right. D'ye think it's decent to show your bum to everybody? "

" Rosalie! Make haste and put some cream on my bottom! "

" Do you suppose I'm servant to your backside? If it smarts you a little, so much the better. It'll make a nicer girl of you. "

" Oh, good little Rosy, do please ! "

" Go to the devil ! " shouted the servant. Then, as if regretting her coarse, but lively rejoinder, she added in kinder tones : " Well, where's your cold cream pot ? And I say, you know, look out so that your pa don't see you ! "

The little girl and her nurse went towards a small round building, covered with ivy, which was no doubt the private retreat of the villa, but Rosalie had scarcely opened the door halfway when she was called.

" Where are you going, Rosalie ? " shouted from the top of the steps the individual I had just seen playing the part of the flogging father. " Isn't Jennie big enough to be able to do her jobs alone ? What have you got in your hand ? Ah ! I guess—you're going to rub some grease or the other over her backside. I forbid that, you hear ? If I've whipped her, it's not that

she may be at her ease.   Let her feel the pain
as long as possible. "

Rosalie and Jennie went back into the house,
with downcast looks, the little girl murmuring
under her breath, and throwing a wicked glance
at her father.   Then all became silent in the
neighbouring garden once more.

This little scene had amused me, on account
of the sensual gracefulness of the child, and it
afforded me satisfaction to draw from memory
in my sketch-book, certain attitudes that had
struck my fancy.   I was making a rapid picture
of pretty Jennie on the trapeze, when I heard
a knock at the door leading into the side-alley.
At first I paid no heed to the rapping, but as
the noise did not cease, I went to the window,
and looked out to see who was disturbing me.
I perceived a young woman, most elegantly
dressed, and whose face was lifted towards my
open casement.   Our eyes met.   She smiled,

and I returned an answering laugh. She
seemed to me to be extremely pretty, and I
had not the slightest hesitation in opening the
door to her, hoping that if she were not
applying in mistake, as I was bound to suppose,
I should nevertheless be able to frame some
excuse to inveigle her into the pavilion.

I was not disappointed when I found myself
face to face with her. Her figure was slight
and well-proportioned, with large hips. She
possessed the dark eyes of a loving woman
greedy of caresses, and everything in her face
and body seemed to breath promising hopes of
pleasure and lust.

" Excuse me, sir, " she said, " if I come
and trouble you, but I should like to have a
martinet which has fallen into your garden.
Look, " she added, glancing through the glass
door, " I fancy I can see it. There, to the
right, near the wall. "

" Take a seat, madame, I pray you, " I said, conducting her into a sitting-room. " I will go and fetch it. "

She wanted to remain standing in the entrance, but I led her gently to a sofa, and ran to pick up the martinet which I had seen fall near a cluster of young cedars.

" No doubt, " said I, inwardly, " this is the mother or the stepmother of little Jennie. I wonder if she is as cruel as her husband ? "

These questions I put to myself as I lifted the teazing instrument I had been asked for off the ground. The strips of tough leather, each terminating in a knot, seemed more fitted to tan the hide of some mutinous sailor boy, than to punish the venial errors of a delicate and graceful child. There were brown stains here and there on the thongs.

I came back to the young woman, who rose

on my entrance, and held out her hand to take
the martinet.

"I am not going to give it you, madame,"
said I, with merry irony, "unless you promise
me never again to use it for barbarous chastisement. You are too charming, and seem too
good ever to flourish a whip over pretty
backsides, especially if such should belong to
any near relatives."

She blushed and tried to laugh.

"But, sir, martinets are not always destined
to correct naughty children. You know very
well that clothes, curtains, and carpets are
beaten with them. They are very handy."

"I know a few things," I replied, "that
you may not know, and which you may doubtless be happy to learn. Shall I tell them?"

"What do you mean?" she asked, rather
astonished.

"I begged her to come upstairs, where we

should be much more comfortable, and to help
her to make up her mind, I went on :

" I shan't give it up to you, if you refuse to
listen to me. "

But she was already going up the stairs.
We went into my room, and I showed her the
sketches.   She recognised the source of my
inspiration.

" Good heavens ! " she exclaimed.   " He has
been whipping her again ! "   She continued,
as she sat down : " You must look upon me as
a monster.   Believe me, that when I asked you
for the martinet, it was out of pity for my poor
child.   Hear me out, for I should be shocked
if you took me to be a wicked woman.   My
daughter is a giddy hoyden, and the country
air gets into her head and makes her very
difficult to keep within bounds.   You smile
because I call Le Perreux the country, but for
us who have lived in Paris so many years

without leaving it for a day, we fancy ourselves in some free region. We might be in the wilds of America, in the Far West, and we fancy every minute that we are going to be attacked by savages. My little Jennie has become an untamable wild girl in this suburban retreat. As for me, sir, I must tell you that I was born among poor people in the quarter of the central markets, and our mothers think nothing of pulling down our drawers and applying their broomsticks. We felt a little shame and some itching for a day or so, and truly it made us better behaved. I do to Jennie what my mamma did to me. From time to time my tomboy comes in for slight spanking. If fashionable ladies bring up their children in more gentle style, I do not blame them, but I was not harmed by being educated under the rod, and see nothing wrong in my pet being thrashed as I was. But her father is a real executioner. He does not correct her—he martyrises her. He fancies that she is not his child, and he vents on my little girl all the rage he feels against me, and which he does not dare to let me see, because at bottom he is very cowardly. That is why I asked you for the wretched whip. With it, he can hurt her greatly, but the pain is transitory. Anyhow he will not maim her, but if he gets it into his head to flog her, and cannot find the martinet, he will strike her with anything that comes first to his hand—an iron bar; or a loaded cane—at the risk of killing her! It is horrible to think of, but that man is always out of temper. He hardly gets home from Paris, where he is employed by a railway company, when he begins to grumble, scold, and always finds some excuse in his fury to fall foul of the child. When he first began to beat Jennie, I tried to come between them. He frightened me so that I no longer dared. But you don't know what splendid vengeance I invented! I got one of my female friends to write him an anonymous letter where it was set forth that I betrayed him, and that he only had to come home at a certain day and hour, and catch me with my accomplice. Instead of returning as usual at seven o'clock in the evening, he applied for leave and appeared here suddenly in the afternoon. I got plenty fun out of his surprise and disappointed looks. I recommenced the practical joke five or six times, and he has never guessed how he has been fooled. He was extremely angry, quite certain at one moment that I was unfaithful, and then wished to believe in my innocence. These ups and downs of doubt and confidence made me extremely joyful. Ah! were I not an honest woman, when he thus castigates my poor infant; when he outrages me by insulting his own flesh and blood, how I should like to really outrage him, and efface all his wretched kisses in one ardent, voluptuous, passionate pressure of other lips that—Ah ! what have I said ? "

" Something that gives me cruel ideas. "

" I do not understand you, " she replied, in a tone of voice that proved she was trying to appear indifferent.

At this juncture, loud cries were heard in the neighbouring villa. We both rushed to the window, and I saw little Jennie running with drawers halfway down her legs, and her skirts uplifted. Her eyes were haggard, and her hair flying in the breeze. Her father, in his shirt sleeves, his features lighted up with an expression even more ferocious than I had noted before, pursued her, brandishing a wet napkin.

" So, crocodile, you wanted to be revenged? Well, my girl, I'm not yet tired of giving you a dose or two of sound thrashing. You can have as múch flogging as you like. I'm on hand whenever you want me. Rosalie! Catch her for me, can't you?"

The obedient servant girl had intercepted Jennie in her flight, and held her tightly in the proper posture, so that the wee cheeks of the child's tender bottom should be advantageously exposed to the paternal punishment, and not a blow be lost. The little martyr howled in most gruesome fashion.

"Ah! *mon Dieu!*" cried Jennie's mother at my elbow. "·I can't look on. It makes me feel sick!"

I sat next to her, as close as possible, inhaling the perfume of her body, enjoying the view of her palpitating bosom, upon which I placed both hands, moulding her breasts, and then I pressed her large posteriors.

" Do you remember, dear madame, what words escaped you just now? "

" What did I say? "

" That you would like to be revenged on that cruel man. "

The wild shrieks of the little girl could still be heard, preceded and followed by the sharp, cracking sound of the damp linen striking her naked flesh.

The young wife clasped my head in her two hands and inclined her supple frame towards me with an undulating movement of her hips, and then she shook her luxuriant dark hair over her eyes as if to veil her features. I clutched her roughly, and we became one, as my body joined hers, and I forced an entrance into her. She bounded under my strokes, as if possessed by the devil, and I accompanied my kisses with every kind of refined caress, sucking her lips, and pinching her vast, rotund hinder charms, as I engulphed my organ of virility deeper and deeper into her greedy, clinging cleft of lust.

She bit my mouth through her forest of hair, and with sighs of delight, held me to her in like manner, squeezing my loins and backside with the same libidinous curiosity.

In the garden, Jennie still sobbed and moaned as we relaxed our embrace.

"Quick!" exclaimed my mistress of a minute, as she drew herself up erect; and quite coldly, as if nothing had passed between us, she added : "Quick! Give me a comb! I want to put my hair to rights. You see now that if I had taken home the martinet, he would not have hurt her so much." Then, running to the window, she went on : "Poor little thing! How she's crying! Her tiny bum is quite raw!"

Her splendid locks were promptly in order, and she smoothed down the creases of her skirt.

" Never mind, " she said, as if speaking to herself, " I've made him a fine cuckold, and no mistake—the rotten beast! "

I considered it my duty now to lavish all sorts of insipid compliments upon her, although I was genuinely happy, and grateful for her unexpected visit.

" What a delicious surprise you granted me! May I hope soon to see you again ? "

She did not answer me, but ran downstairs hurriedly without forgetting to take her martinet.

On the threshold, I wanted to kiss her, but she eluded my embrace. All she would do was just to touch my hand with the tips of her fingers, and reply to my eager " good bye " and proffered mouth by rapidly skimming over my moustache with her closed lips. She fled like a hare, leaving the sweet fragrance of lilies of the valley behind her.

I went back up the stairs to my room to witness her return to her home.

She made her entry laughing and singing. Her husband, as a rest from flagellation, was watering the flower-beds.

" It was bound to happen, tra la la !   You are in a nice state now, tra la la ! " she warbled.

" What's the matter with you ?   Are you mad ? " he replied, without ceasing his man-œuvres with the watering-can.   " I don't like to see you in this mood.   Anybody would think you had taken a drop too much.   You're tipsy ! "

" How polite you are ! I merely remark that your forehead is covered with perspiration, and that you do wrong to work so hard in the hot sun. "

*
* *

I must have looked very funny when I dined

that evening with my host, for he said to me,
laughing and rubbing his hands :

" You appear as triumphant as if you had
been lucky in love ! "

He so pressed me with questions that I wound
up by confessing my adventure.

" Well, " said he, " your rival is seated
opposite you—oh ! a very ancient one.   Now,
the lady don't even trouble to look at me.
This is how I had her. I noticed last year
when I came to live here, that my pretty neighbour was always in a good humour with me
when her husband had given his little girl a
good slap-bottom. I, in my pavilion, and she,
in her garden, began chatting together. We
were both of one opinion : pitying the child
and blaming its father, who, happily, once his
ideas of disciplinary justice satisfied, would
shut himself up indoors, and not show his ugly
face any more.   As his young wife was exactly

to my taste, these conversations only half satisfied my longings. I bribed that sweet person, Rosalie, to get up some big childish peccadillo, which was to appear in the father's eyes as if committed by his daughter, and thus draw down upon her some terrible punishment. The same evening, esconced in the pavilion you are now occupying, I soon heard a great noise of blows, raging voices, and yells of pain. The din subsided, or I should say, diminished. The sound of swishing strokes gave way to an impassioned dialogue that lasted far into the night, and at last the villa became quiet. I thought that husband, wife, and child were at rest and asleep, when I heard a knocking at the door in the alley. I went down, and saw my dear next-door friend, Jennie's mamma. She was in her chemise, her only other garment being a large fur cape without fastenings, leaving her legs and shoulders bare.

" Oh! " she cried, " protect me, save me!
My husband is a monster ! He has just flayed
my poor child alive.   I will never again live
under his roof. "

In short, to show how she had deserted him,
she slept with me until the morning, and I
enjoyed one of the best nights of love I ever
remember.

" Would you believe that since then, although
she did not seem to be displeased with my
talents, she never once returned to see me.
Better still, she has never even spoken to me.
When we meet in the alley, or strolling about
the village, which often happens, she turns her
face away, and pretends she has not seen me.
Strange creature!   Still I hope you will be
luckier than I was ! "

But my adventure was exactly the same as that
of my client. I did not see the father again,
kept in Paris, or perhaps forced to travel for his

employers.   Little Jennie often suffered from
a sore bottom, but the slaps of her mamma or
the servant were not very frightful, and if the
girl yelled or wept, it was no doubt more from
temper and shame than from pain.   As for her
mother, she never looked in the direction of my
window. We often met, when I would bow,
and pay her a few compliments, but she did not
answer, never even betraying by the least sign
that she had seen me. I bought over Rosalie,
giving her often a gold piece, and even two or
three bank-notes, so that she might read my
passionate letters to her mistress, plead my cause
with her, and become my go-between, but she
always returned to me with my envelopes unopened, saying dolefully : " Madame won't
hear a word about you."

" Strange creature ! "   I said to myself,
repeating my host's expression.

After all, she had given herself once to me so

frankly and completely that she left nothing more for my desire to long for. I should have preferred to renew that adorable intertwining embrace, although it would no longer have savoured of surprise, as the perfume of lilies of the valley of her jacket and armpits; the delicate wild strawberry flavour of her melting lips; the vast, firm plenitude of her buttocks; the forest of her beautiful hair, and especially the indescribable grace, awkwardness, and amorous fury of her yielding grip had transported me to the seventh heaven of delight. But such enjoyments cannot be renewed. Once experienced, we must, at the same time as we feel them, commit them to our memory, embalming them in our remembrance, to serve now and again as delicious pictures with which to accompany other ordinary pleasures, that without such help would be less perfect, and incomplete.

VICTIMS OF LOVE

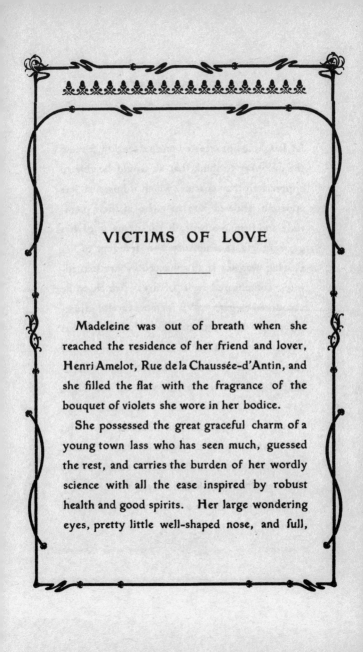

VICTIMS OF LOVE

———

Madeleine was out of breath when she reached the residence of her friend and lover, Henri Amelot, Rue de la Chaussée-d'Antin, and she filled the flat with the fragrance of the bouquet of violets she wore in her bodice.

She possessed the great graceful charm of a young town lass who has seen much, guessed the rest, and carries the burden of her wordly science with all the ease inspired by robust health and good spirits. Her large wondering eyes, pretty little well-shaped nose, and full, fat, laughing lips arrested one's attention, forcing the onlooker to think that he would be able to appreciate other charms, which if however less apparent, allowed him to guess at their plenitude and firmness beneath the drapery of her garments. The simplicity and freedom of her bearing was not at all enhanced by her exceedingly complicated style of dress, which to be accounted elegant, called for more careful adjustment and less exuberance. Madeleine's hat was all awry, and her hair touzled, as if she had just got out of bed. Beneath the bolero-shaped jacket, her skirt, hooked up too high, yawned open behind, and to complete everything, her natty boots, lace-flounced frock, and silk petticoat were covered with stains of mud. Madeleine must have dismissed her cab. Perhaps the spendthrift lass had not even the necessary bit of silver to take a hired vehicle, and had come on foot.

Henri Amelot had just lost his wife, when he fell across this savoury, ripe morsel of lust, as if just in time to console him and divert his sad thought from grief. Love had followed on a chance fancy.   At the moment when this little tale begins, the hours that he passed in company of his mistress were the only bright ones of his existence.   He entirely neglected his daughter, little Séverine, a child of about ten years of age, who had been all in all to him once.   Most of his money—and he was a rich man—passed into Madeleine's pocket, and she was always greedy for gold,. without avarice, wickedness, or luxurious tastes.

" Well ! Are you not going to kiss me ? " she asked, offering her fresh and rosy cheek.

Henri replied to this amiable invitation by pressing his mouth to his sweetheart's lips and face, but without eagerness, as merely from habit.   He appeared very troubled and annoyed.

" What ails you? Why do you pull such a long face? "

" Madeleine," said he, " I have been expecting you for the last fortnight. Why did you not come to see me? Why have you not answered any of my letters ? "

" What do you mean? Your letters? I only received one, wherein you told me that you were leaving Paris and would only return to-day. "

" Did I write that? "

" Certainly. I've got your note in my pocket. There, see for yourself. "

" It looks like my handwriting, " said Henri, vastly surprised. " Yet I am sure I never wrote this to you. I am not a somnambulist ! What wretch has dared to forge my name and copy my writing? You have a lover ! "

" There you go again ! Your foolish ideas spring up once more ! "

" I'm not mad. You have a lover, I say. "

" If you like ! "

" And you show him my letters ! "

" We read them together in bed, every night. "

" Madeleine ! " exclaimed Henri, seizing her wrists, " do not laugh and joke. It might bring you bad luck. "

" Let me go ! You're most absurd ! " she rejoined, shrugging her sloping shoulders. " If you so greatly desired my visit only to make a scene, I should have done better to have stopped at home. "

Henri grew suddenly calm, and his voice changed to a tone of supplication.

" Madeleine, if I'm jealous, it's because I love you. "

" Yes, yes, I know, you all say that ! But as for me, I warn you, I don't like to be worried, and have you always on top of me. "

"Because you want your liberty, so as to be free to do the first foolish thing that comes into your head. If I thought you were not faithful to me, I don't know what I'd do!"

Madeleine smiled. Her friend's tragical outbursts always afforded her great amusement.

"Henri," she said in grave accents, "mother is coming to see me at five o'clock this evening, and I should not like the dear old thing to have to trudge uselessly from Belleville to the Champs Elysées. That's a bit of a journey, you know! So just see if you haven't got something better to do than to stand there jabbering away, as I must soon be off."

"Couldn't you have made an appointment with your mother for some other day?"

"I didn't know you would have been at home to-day. I only knew of your arrival through this wire."

" A telegram from me? All this is very extraordinary. "

" Oh! don't start your suppositions again, " said Madeleine, " it's awfully tiring. Some friend has been playing practical jokes : that's certain. Undress me, and think no more about it. "

He forgot his suspicions for a moment in the face of Madeleine's fresh young beauty, as with fervent lips he paid homage to every charm that was gradually unveiled and revealed to his sight. First the breasts received his kisses, and then her pretty proudly-curving posteriors which she offered him with a silvery laugh. He knelt before them.

" Have you been beaten? " he asked. " Your bottom is scratched all over. "

" Whoever do you think has beaten me? Mamma? I think I've passed the age of spankings. Yesterday I went to see a lady friend at Asnières, and I fell off the swing in her garden. There was a lot of new gravel just put down, and that's why my bum is rather red."

They went to bed, but had hardly got between the sheets when both started up in fright.

" What in the world is in these sheets?" exclaimed Madeleine.

" How should I know?"

" It looks just as if they were full of cow-itch."

" There's some demon in the house!"

" Your lady's maid is having larks with you, that's sure! I'm itching all over!" said Madeleine, twisting her shoulders about, and her entire frame writhing.

Henri suggested that she should take a bath to calm the irritation, but the pipes were evidently being repaired, as all the taps had been unscrewed.

"Who could have done this?" Henri said to himself. "I had my bath this morning and everything was all right then."

Madeleine went into the dressing-room where she washed herself all over and then gave her dress to be brushed to the lady's maid who brought it back to her a few minutes later.

"This is maddening!" she suddenly exclaimed, raging furiously. "Look! The lace flounce has been taken off, and the bottom has been cut with a scissors. What's going on in your place?"

Henri called the lady's maid and gave her a severe scolding.

"I don't know what master is finding fault with me for," replied the girl with marked astonishment, showing her sincerity. "I brought back Madame's dress, directly I had done brushing it. Pauline made the bed, and cleaned the bath-room. She's too old not to know better than to play such silly jokes. ''

'' Where's Séverine? Tell her to come here! ''

'' I haven't seen mademoiselle to-day. No doubt she has remained at her little friend's house. ''

'' Dear boy, '' said Madeleine, '' I can't go away in this state. My dress isn't fit to be seen. Run quick and buy me some lace like the rest. Your lady's maid won't know where to go to match it, and she'll be too frightened to give the price. I don't know either what it will cost you. It'll perhaps be dear enough, but as my frock has been torn at your place, it's only right that you should pay for it. ''

Henri took the remainder of the lace and went out at once.

Madeleine, while awaiting her friend's return,

started strolling through the entire flat, like
some impertinent little lassie who is at home
wherever she may be. In this way, she soon
reached young Séverine's bed-room, where, for
want of something better to do, she turned
over a copybook on the table.

The first few leaves were devoted to history
lessons, but afterwards she was astounded to
find at the end a rough sketch of a letter, in
quite a different handwriting, and which strongly
resembled that of her lover. " My dear
Madeleine, I am forced to leave Paris for a
fortnight "—the very words of the note she had
received ! At the side of the inkstand was
an envelope, whereon Henri Amelot had
scribbled a few lines, and by comparing this
writing with the page of the exercise book,
Madeleine thought that both, seemingly identical at first sight, were really not by the same
hand. Had Séverine been imitating her

father's script, or one of her professors? No, the little girl was the only culprit. Madeleine doubted no longer, when continuing to rummage in the room, she spyed out at the back of a drawer, a box of cow-itch and the piece of lace that had been cut off her dress.

" Oh! what a jade! Oh, the little minx! " she exclaimed. " And only think that I brought her cakes and chocolate! Wasn't I a fool? She's at home now perchance. The lady's maid has misled us. Henri's daughter can't be out, for she only cut the lace away just now. Oh! if I could put my hand on her! I'd teach her to make fun of me! "

She once more proceeded on her search in every room, when suddenly, thinking of the water-closet, she dashed into it rapidly. The door of the passage shut to with a bang, and she heard another door that gave on to the servant's staircase opened quickly. But Made-

leine was as lively as a bird.   Before Séverine
had   time to escape, her father's mistress
caught her by her short skirt, and dragged the
child back by the ear to the seat of the privy.
By main force, the enraged woman bent her
over it.

The little girl's confusion, blushes, and silence
proved her guilt up to the hilt.   She did not
dare make a movement, whilst Madeleine slipped a hand under her petticoats to pull off her
tiny knickers.   No doubt the guilty girlie
thought it was useless to struggle against
Madeleine, and it were better that the chastisement should remain a secret.   Her heart beat
hurriedly, and she stiffened her limbs with all her
might, as if to enable her to support the coming
strokes without crying out.   Madeleine seized
the usual little broom that is kept in these
needful retreats, and rained down on her naked
buttocks a shower of blows quite sufficient to

have caused a less courageous child to howl
with pain. When Madeleine noticed the first
drops of blood, she ceased hitting her victim
with the malodorous instrument and let Séverine go.

"You can complain to your pa," she then
said, "if you want some more!"

Séverine had not uttered a shriek, nor heaved
a sigh, but Madeleine had no sooner concluded
her threat, than the tiny vixen spat on the
bosom of her dress.

Madeleine left her with a gesture of contempt.
She was in such a passion that she did not even
wait for her lover's return, but went off with
her torn skirt, after having asked the lady's
maid for five francs to pay for her cab.

She had not been gone a minute when Henri
came back. He was very much put out when
told that Madeleine was no longer there.
Seeing little Séverine crimson with emotion,

and self-contained pain, he felt inclined to vent his rage on her.

" Ah! there you are!" he shouted at his daughter, pulling her rougly to him. "I should like to know who spoilt Madame Madeleine's dress, and got up to vile tricks in my room?"

He then reproached her with all the petty crimes she had committed, causing him to suffer with his friend, the lady visitor.

Séverine lifted towards her father her beautiful bright eyes, which appeared as if they could only express kindness, frankness, and love, as she said with simplicity :

" I did it all, papa!"

" Wretched child!" exclaimed Henri, more surprised than vexed at such an answer.

" Yes, " Séverine went on, " and I am wild at only having been able to annoy her. I wanted to hurt her—the dirty woman who dared to lift her hand to me!"

She stopped short, not wishing to confess that she had been whipped by Madeleine.

"Oh, she beat you, did she?" rejoined Henri. "She was right. You deserved twenty thrashings. That's why you hate her so?"

"No, not for that, but because she gets all your love, and you don't care a straw for me, ever since she came here."

"My poor Séverine, have you lost your wits?" said Henri, bending over the little girl to kiss her.

"No, no, you don't love me any more," continued Séverine, eluding her father's caresses, "you have sacrificed me for a wicked creature!"

"I forbid you to talk in that way, Séverine," said Henri severely.

"She's a bad woman, and she isn't fond of you now," rejoined the daughter. "I'll prove it."

Thereupon, Séverine ran to her room, and returned with a crumpled letter wich bore the address of Madeleine Aubert, Avenue des Champs Elysées, on the envelope. After an interminable chaplet of amorous flattery, and caressing words, the note wound up as follows :

"Try, my own Madelon, to screw some brass out of your Henri No. 1. If you had a few quids in your purse, we might treat ourselves next Sunday to a first-class beano. You know what a dab I am at finding out quiet little naughty corners where we can have some fun and no questions asked.

"Ever thine,
ANDRE."

Henri was now as white as a ghost.

" You—you took this letter out of the skirt of her dress?" he asked, each syllable falling from his lips as if it was a great effort for him to open his mouth.

"Yes, it was pinned underneath. I showed it to Julienne, the lady's maid, and she explained it to me. Says she : ' That there woman doesn't care one least little bit for your poor pa. She only runs after him for his money.'"

But Henri gave no heed to the conclusion of her gossip. He quickly crammed the letter into his pocket, caught up his hat, and made off in the greatest haste.

"I think it's all over now!" said Séverine, jumping for joy.

"What's all over?" asked the lady's maid.

"Pa's love for the dirty woman. I showed him the letter."

"You've gone and done a nice thing!" exclaimed Julienne. "They'll have a row, and as they've both got violent tempers, it'll be far above a joke. I've witnessed awful scenes between them that struck me all of a heap. He's quite capable of killing her."

" A good riddance, if he does. "

" A nice way of settling matters, I must say; but what would happen to him afterwards? You never listen to anybody, and fine things come of your obstinacy. "

Henri had driven off to Madeleine's dwelling, without losing a minute. The young woman opened the door herself. She seemed greatly surprised at seeing him, and at first would not let him enter.

" What's the matter? What has happened to you? You know mother is here. "

" Never mind her, " said he, repulsing her as far as her bed-room. " Do you know this letter? "

Madeleine laughed wickedly and slyly.

" What if I do? " was her tranquil rejoinder. " Did you think I put up with you for love of your fine face—"

She did not conclude her sentence, for Henri

seized her hands, and lifting his walking-stick,
struck her on the shoulders, back, and legs.

"Pity! Pardon!" she ejaculated.

"No! No pity for lying whores!"

She fell groaning on her knees against the
bed. He tore off her dressing-gown, drawers,
and slight chemise, converting the lace that had
cost him so much money into valueless rags,
while he bruised and rendered all bloody the
body of the loved one, whose supple loins, and
the large lower mountains, with their bold, full
symmetrical contours and enticing curves had
once been the enchantment of his eyes.

She moaned and sobbed, but seemed resigned
to her fate, when suddenly rising to her feet,
she ran to the door of her dressing-closet,
and called out with all the strength of her
lungs:

"André! André!"

A rather robust young man, short, sturdy,

and broad-shouldered, came into the room without undue haste.

" Hullo there! D'ye want anybody to lend a hand? Haven't you done whopping the gal? Whose place is this here, after all? You seem to be making yourself at home. You'd better pay the young woman what you owe her! "

He muttered and grumbled between his clenched teeth, but seemed in no hurry to defend Madeleine or punish her agressor, but when Henri began to insult and assault him, he lost his temper.

" Will you clear out, pimp! " cried Henri, seizing him by the collar, and trying to throw him out of the apartment.

The man suddenly turned upon the tricked lover, and gave him a heavy blow of his fist, full in the chest. Henri staggered. Madeleine, who up till then had remained an impassible spectatress, pushed him, trying to trip him up. With her companion's help, she managed to succeed. Henri fell, dragging his adversary with him. The two wrestled for a few moments, closely locked together. Madeleine seized the stick which Henri had let fall, and she struck him with it between the legs. Then, squatting down behind her rich keeper, she squeezed and pressed the secret fleshy nook of manhood, which in happier times had been the means of supreme caresses for her, perhaps arousing her fullest enjoyment.

All at once, Henri uttered a long, unearthly howl of pain. His opponent clutched him by throat, tightening his grasp gradually. The wretched victim's feet kicked at empty space for an instant; his nails dug into the bully's shoulders, and then he remained without a movement.

"You can get up now," said her fancy man to Madeleine.

She rose to her feet, her features livid, and

her breast heaving with the precipitate palpitation of her heart.

"I think we've done the trick!" the brute added. "Don't tremble so. He oughtn't to have hit me. He began the tussle."

"We must not stop here," said Madeleine, with insensate fright. "Let us be off! Away! Away!"

"I'm going to run the rule over him first. As well be hung for a sheep as for a lamb."

"No, no! I won't let you rob him!" cried Madeleine.

"Won't you? There's only one boss here, and that's me!" replied the murderer in accents of authority, as he darted his mastering eyes in hers. "Rather late for delicacy on your part, my fine lady!"

He searched ill-fated Henri's pockets, took his note-case, purse; and tore the rings off the corpse's still warm fingers.

" I've left him his wedding-ring, one louis, and three francs to pay his fare to the next world. They won't be able to say to-morrow in the papers that the motive of the crime was robbery. "

" A truce to joking ! " shuddered Madeleine. " What you've done is horrible ! "

" Allow me, my beauty—what *we've* done, if you please. I don't think I worked the job alone, did I ? "

Madeleine's servants had been allowed a holiday that evening. When they returned to their work next morning, they found Henri Amelot's body in the middle of the drawing-room. At first, they thought it was a case of self-murder, but the disordered state of the apartment, their mistress's absence, and the confession of a young woman to whom Madeleine, maddened with fear, had told her crime, soon unmasked the truth.

The body of the murdered man was conveyed to his flat in the Rue de la Chaussée-d'Antin. When little Séverine saw her father in the arms of Madeleine's servants, and the contracted, grimacing lineaments of the dead man, she burst into a fit of sobbing, following the corpse to the bed on which it was placed. Then she fell on her knees, and covering her father's ice-cold hands with convulsive kisses, she repeated unceasingly :

"My poor papa! My poor papa! I have killed him!"

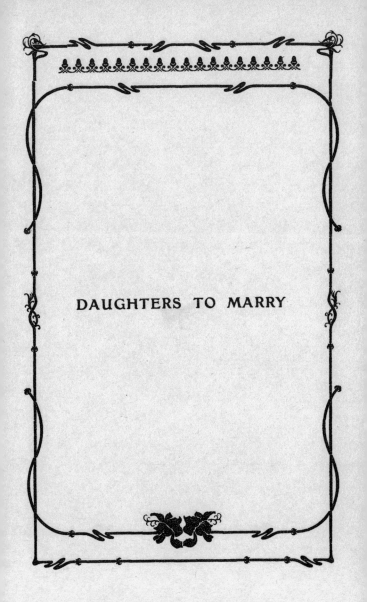

DAUGHTERS TO MARRY

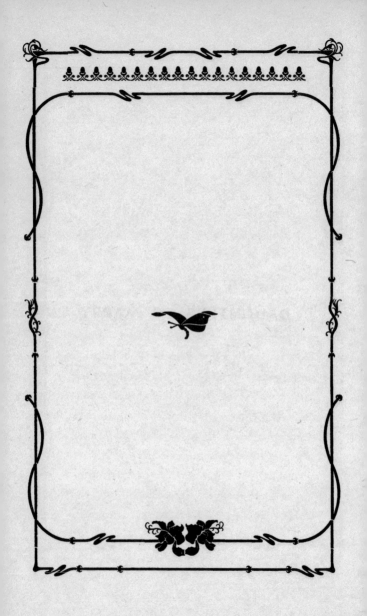

DAUGHTERS TO MARRY

As soon as Henriette Panat had reached her seventeenth year, her mother began thinking about making some grand match. Poor mammas suffer greatly from the terrible fear that their daughters may be left on their hands, and if they had their own way, would busy themselves negotiating the marriage of their middle-class offspring like royal princesses, when still in the cradle. Henriette was a pretty girl, there was no doubt about it. To speak vulgarly, she looked "all there" as far as love was concerned.

She possessed that voluptuous look in her eyes, which at first seems insolent, and when it is accompanied by beautiful hair and a fine figure, commands respect, as well as calling forth desire, and exacerbating and establishing it. With the certainty of a rich dowry, bearing the name of Panat, which three generations of honest merchants had rendered illustrious at Limoges, there was no danger of her becoming an old maid. It seemed as if she did not require to await the arrival of suitors, but would only have to choose amidst a crowd of them. What might make her marriage more difficult was that her mother would not hear of any affianced adorer unless he had millions. He was to be intelligent too, clever in business; as handsome as possible, and above all with the habits of a saint, the vigour of Hercules, the watchful care of a sister of charity, and the amorous passion of Romeo. She had sought for this rare specimen of manhood at Limoges in vain. Without feeling discouraged, she thought she might drop on her ideal somewhere else, and perhaps at the Eaux-Bonnes, a health resort where her doctor had advised her to go.

" Are there any swell people there? " asked this worthy mother, infatuated with ideas of worldly grandeur and betrothed heroes.

Her doctor mentioned the names of counts, dukes, princes, and Parisian and foreign celebrities—all announced in the daily papers as leaving for the Eaux-Bonnes—and Madame Panat, full of hope, began to pack up, and told her daughter to prepare for the journey.

On the day of departure grave cares hung over the house of Panat. It happened that there was not only one daughter in this family, Henriette, but also another little maiden, Georgette. She was rather a big girl, close upon fifteen, and good air coupled with wholesome food had already shaped her into quite a miniature woman. It could easily be seen that she possessed well-developed, fleshy charms under her short frock, and although she only reached to her sister's shoulder, perched on as yet high, thin legs, she was a hardy, healthy, fragrant blossom, and ready for Cupid's harvest. For such as like full descriptions, we may add that she ressembled her sister, but was not so dark, and did not have her haughty, disdainful glance. But she was gifted with more amiable grace, showing that with the best disposition in the world, she was unable to control the impatient vivacity of her pretty frame. This darling, with her angelic eyes, hid a mischievous demon under her petticoats, as the sequel will show.

Georgette, not being of marriageable age, remained entirely forgotten by her family. Madame Panat troubled more about her dog.

The little girl came home on her summer
holiday from the convent school where she
was a boarder all the year round.   She arrived
without many prizes, but making much joyful
noise, and Madame Panat, after kissing her
forehead, continued to carry from her cupboards
and stuff into her boxes, hats, linen, and
frocks, while Henriette answered all her sister's
questions with one laconic sentence, pronounced in haughty, important and mysterious
accents :

" I am going to the Eaux-Bonnes with
mamma. "

" You're off? " exclaimed Georgette. " Then
I'm left all alone? "

" You'll remain with your papa, " said
Madame Panat, not without majesty.

" It happens, " interrupted Monsieur Panat,
" that I have just received a telegram from one
of my branches that will force me to leave

home for a few days. We can't leave Georgette alone here, with maid-servants of whom we are not sure. You ought to take her with you. "

" Take her with us! " exclaimed Madame Panat, as if she had been asked to carry the house on her back.

" She'll be a great trouble when travelling, " said Henriette regretfully, but in quite a proper and solemn sort of way, as befitted a young person who expected soon to be elevated to matrimonial dignity.

She glanced with condescending pity on the hoyden, who knew nothing of the world, and was still studying her spelling, grammar, and arithmetic.

A long discussion now took place between Monsieur and Madame Panat. Mademoiselle Henriette watched the case, her lithe figure languidly leaning sideways, but her chin well forward, ready to throw in a word; while at the end of the room, behind the luggage, Georgette waited for the verdict. Finally, after a bustling trio which lasted nearly an hour, Madame Panat briefly announced to her youngest daughter the resolution of the family council.

" You go with us. "

Georgette uttered cries of enthusiastic joy, forgetting for the time being that during the discussion she had been examining a delicious hat sent expressly from Paris for her sister, and that she was still holding it in her hand. She danced and jumped about in a way that foreboded danger for the fragile, flimsy and expensive headdress.

" What a plague you are! Take that! " cried Henriette, seeing the threatening ruin of the masterpiece of fashion, and boxing her sister's ears in a rage. Georgette was on the point of paying Henriette back in her own coin, when the vast and peaceful bosom of Madame Panat was interposed between the combatants.

" Keep quiet! " she said in severe accents to her youngest daughter.

" But she began! "

" Hold your tongue! She's your elder. You owe her respect. Remember that you haven't left the house yet. I shall take you back to the convent. "

" They don't keep any boarders during the holidays. "

" They would take you, if I desired, " replied Madame Panat, with the gesture of a queen.

" Ah! we're doing very wrong to let her come with us, " sighed Henriette. " What a trouble she'll be! "

" I know that, my child, but what are we to do? Your father wishes it! "

The boxes were packed and locked, final

instructions given, the last farewell uttered, and the three feminine travellers passed through Limoges in their carriage driven with all speed. The eldest daughter took the tickets herself, and chose her own compartment.

Georgette had hardly entered the railway carriage, the train being on the point of leaving the station, when she stretched herself at full length on her stomach along the seat.

" I shall have a nice nap like this, " she said.

" Can't you behave decently, Georgette? " exclaimed Henriette, severely. " Will you get up? "

As her sister did not hurry to obey her, she applied, quite seriously and with her full strength, a tremendous slap on the plump backside that Georgette was unlucky enough to present so commodiously.

Georgette started up at once, rubbing her bottom, blushing for shame at having been

assaulted on that part of the body, like a
little baby school child in the lowest class. She
made a movement of wounded pride and revolt,
shrugging her shoulders, and muttering under
her breath some rather disparaging remarks
concerning her sister.

Henriette nodded her head with an air of
decision, and smiled out of window at nothing
particular, delighted at her act of authority.

As for Madame Panat, she left all the care
and responsibility of direction and judicial
control to her eldest daughter. When this
little scene was enacted she fanned herself with
indifference, full of pride in her motherly
destiny which led her to the Eaux-Bonnes to
get her child married. She gradually worked
her fan less and less, shut up the waving
instrument, twiddled it an instant in her dumpy
hand, and became impassible, her mouth wide
open to admit every kind of dream.

" Ma's asleep, so perhaps you'll keep silent, "
shouted the eldest beauty to her sister, in a
voice loud enough to awake a regiment, but
which was not heard by the sleeping woman.

Rather frightened by this sister of hers who
was so handy with her slaps, Georgette huddled
herself up in front of her mother, and dropped
into sound slumber almost at the word of
command.   Before Henriette dropped off,
she enjoyed a good, long " think " all about
the charming acquaintances she was about to
make, and passed in review artless seductive
tactics.

At the Eaux-Bonnes, they were soon known
to everybody on the parade.   The morning,
returning from the bath; the afternoon, leaving
the Hotel de France, when lunch was over,
and in the evening after dinner, Madame Panat
led her eldest daughter along.   When we say
she led her, it is not quite the truth.   It was

more Mademoiselle who led her mother. This
was the order of the procession : George went
first, skirmishing, her nose in the air, three
camp-stools under her arm, walking on both
sides of the path at once. Next came Henriette,
with slow steps, her parasol over her shoulder,
carrying her head high, and her eyelids low;
her figure braced up and her posteriors strapped
down, pressed and rounded by her narrow
skirt, surmounted by a bodice in the latest
style of 1901, advancing like a queen in a
ballet *cortège*. Madame her mother brought
up the rear, fat and short, out of breath, under
a violet, monumental hat, on which were fixed
vast, nodding plumes. She followed hurrying,
but never fast enough to get level with her
eldest child, who was obliged to stop and wait
for her. When at last, puffing and blowing,
with pains in her knees, Madame Panat caught
up her daughter, Henriette would turn round

and show her mother her face full of heavy reproach and bad temper, as she hissed out a " Whatever are you about, ma? " which overwhelmed the worthy dame with shame.

The cause of the eldest girl's " moods " was that she had not got engaged as soon as she stepped out of the train, and when ten long days had passed, was still waiting for the appearance of a loving sweetheart.

" And yet I'm pretty ! " she said to herself night and morning, as she looked in the glass on retiring to rest and on arising.

What sights—scarcely decent according to ideas of modern pudicity, but right pleasant for all votaries of the female undraped frame—the lucky mirror of room No. 125 reflected daily! How Henriette contemplated her shape, naked and dressed ! How she turned and twisted about in front of the glass, comparing herself to the women of Limoges, or those stopping at her hotel! She had even gone so far as to buy portraits of actresses, and artistic photographs of naked females, so as to study her own beauty, enhance it, and give it prominence, without sparing herself. She tried by all kinds of artifices if it were not possible to repair a few of nature's imperfections.

"It is your fault, ma," she said one morning to the woman who had brought her into the world, "if I look like some poor guy of a governess at the Casino, with the few wretched frocks I've got. You must really let me have a tailor-made costume, and you will have to buy me some lace for my dinner blouse."

"But, my dear child," said Madame Panat, "we shall be short of cash."

"Write to papa."

"He'll be furious. Besides, a new dress can't be ready for a week or ten days, and you know we are off at the end of August. It isn't worth while to be so extravagant for such a short time."

"All right, mother," answered the eldest darling, and for the next two days she only unlocked her lips to reply to her mother's anxious demands as to what ailed her, "there's absolutely nothing the matter with me!" in accents which allowed it to be guessed that she was suffering unspeakable torture, or else to shout to her sister, when she heard her sing or laugh, "Shut up, you unnerve me! If you're not quiet, I'll slap your face!"

Matersamilias put a serious question to herself. Would the grief of not having the desired falbalas render her darling daughter dumb? But at this critical juncture, on a certain evening, the thirteenth they had passed at the Eaux-Bonnes, a young man, of most charming appearance, with an elegant fair moustache, took his seat at the *table d'hôte* next to Henriette, and began to pass the dishes to the young girl with amiable gallantry, now and again making play with long and amorous side-glances, while he tried by a thousand decently discreet and generally commonplace questions to get into conversation with her.

Mademoiselle Henriette, without hiding the immense joy she felt at this long-expected torrent of masculine attentions, was however too troubled to reply to these bold advances. She was far from being loquacious, but compensated herself for her restraint when she rose from table and was alone with her mother. She did not hide her enthusiasm, and forgetting her primitive reserve, gradually reached such heights that Madame Panat, frightened at this sudden outburst of sensual passion, although always submissive to her eldest girl's will, declared that she would make enquiries about the young man, without the least delay.

" If his character is good, as I hope, my pet, I will leave him full liberty to court you. "

" But ma, " said Henriette, " attentions mean nothing ! "

" That's where you're wrong ! He must not compromise you. "

They did all they could to get to know something about the handsome young man, or rather they tried hard, but little can be gleaned about anybody from strangers in a watering-place who only know each other from the day of arrival and meeting.

" He looks honest, " said Madame Panat, tired of vain questioning and desirous not to be scolded by her daughter. " I shall let them become friendly. It will always be time enough to prevent a disadvantageous marriage. Anyhow, I'm there to watch over them ! "

From that moment, the fair young Prince Charming who called himself Count Albert

Dugazon, never left Henriette all day. The young girl hung on his slightest utterance with more rapt attention than the most devout woman had ever granted to a favourite preacher. On her campstool, in the shade of spreading acacias, Madame Panat often had inward misgivings.

" I've got my eye on them, " she would then mumble to cheer herself up, without recollecting how from time to time the heat of the sun caused her head to droop on her shoulder, and forced her eyelids to drop heavily down.

" Let him say what he likes to you, " was her advice to Henriette, when they held their matutinal councils of war, for at night the poor lady was so tired that she fell asleep while undressing. " But don't let him touch or kiss you. Young men take such liberties! Fancy he is an Adonis and extremely amiable, if you like, but never let him know you think so. "

" Don't be alarmed, ma, " replied Henriette,

with a disdainful and conceited smile. " I know how to play my cards. "

Nevertheless, the young schemer felt quite inclined to allow Albert much more freedom than her mamma deemed right to authorise. Unfortunately, Georgette, like some guardian angel or devil, always turned up at the most touching moments.

" Will you be off? " Henriette would impatiently shriek at her.

" Ma told me to stop with you two! " Georgette would retort, with great innocent eyes and a smile that belied her glance.

" You little wretch! " was her elder sister's rejoinder.

Henriette, on reaching home in the evening, slipped one hand up her sister's petticoats, and traitrously pinched her buttocks, so cruelly, that her poor little victim's eyes filled with tears.   But this took place in a corridor of the

hotel, among waiters and travellers coming and
going, so Georgette had to stifle her desire to
pay Henriette back in kind, contenting herself
with clenching her fists and murmuring between
her teeth, as she fled up the stairs :

" Never mind, I'll have my revenge one
day ! "

Did Georgette ever glut her desire for vengeance, at any rate in the way she desired?
No one ever knew.   Fortune smiles or frowns
upon us, without our prayers, and despite our
efforts to help the blind goddess.   Georgette,
however, could never have dreamt that one fine
day, of which we are now about to write,
would have terminated so strangely, or that
she would have been the heroine of the hour,
in spite of herself.

Very early that morning a party composed
of a guide, Albert, Henriette, Georgette and
poor Madame Panat had started off on a

mountain excursion. In order to follow and protect her virtuous offspring, this devoted mother worked harder than a recruit at a sham fight, and her maternal campaign equalled in fatigue that of a Kitchener in South Africa.

They had left the Eaux-Bonnes in a big landau the night before, and slept at Gabas. At the first peep of dawn, the ladies, alpenstock in hand, had departed with the two men on their climbing expedition.

We shall not describe the marvellous rosy landscape they saw unrolled before them, the spirals of the woolly mist in the valleys; their sudden surprise when the torrent rolled menacingly almost under their very feet, as it were; the shade of thick woods; the majesty of the yellow rocks; the sheltered nooks where pretty hamlets offered restful halting-places after stony solitudes had been passed; and far away in the distance, the background of blue

mountains, snowy peaks crowned with rays of
light. In the presence of such glorious sights,
it can well be understood that even poor
mamma forgot her fatigue for a time, and kept
on climbing up and up. These ascensions,
however, make one hungry, and our young
ladies were not angelic enough to be satisfied
to feast on a sunrise and a distant view of gla-
ciers. Ten o'clock had hardly struck when
despite their two big breakfast cups of morning chocolate, they were as voracious as she-
wolves, and were not displeased to find that
Albert had anticipated their desires by having
made the guide carry a well-furnished pic-nic
basket containing a truffled fowl, meat-pie,
fruit, and champagne; all of which was eagerly
welcomed. When of the victuals forming the
collation nothing was left but bones and empty
bottles, and everybody had chatted, laughed
heartily, and emptied their glasses, saying,

" What a beautiful view!—How lovely!—This
pie is delicious!—Another little drop of champagne, mademoiselle.— Don't drink so much,
it'll turn acid," and a thousand other remarks in
the same style, they began to think of returning.

They retraced their steps, but not without
difficulties in the way of climbing awkward
places; falls and slips. Madame Panat, in a big
straw hat and a pair of cyclist's bloomers,
advanced slowly, marking her progress with the
drops of her profuse perspiration. She marched
by the side of the guide, fearful of losing
her way, and thereby causing the other excur-
sionists a little delay. Georgette lead the van,
running the risk of having to retrace her steps
when she mistook the path, and as lively as if
she had not scampered over many useless miles
of ground. It was without doubt a most pretty
sight to see her clambering about. Her little,
white, shapely boots pattered along, slipping on

the rocks, and disappearing no one knew where in a heap of loose pebbles. Now and again the plump rotundity of her perfectly formed juvenile buttocks seemed as if offering itself mockingly under the scanty skirt. Then her saucy smiling phiz would peep out from under the shade of her hat, bent down in front, and cocked up behind, above the little golden curls of her hair at each side of the nape of her slight neck, and under the simple silk light-coloured floating blouse which tightened itself on her supple shoulders, the merest vague sketch of two budding breasts could be seen. The upper part of her figure, and the tiny waist, encircled in a leather belt, seemed out of proportion above the swelling backside. But her merry bounds and delicious capers caused an incident which if in olden days might have been glossed over with laugh and joke, in our strange epoch of false shame gave rise to a most dramatic resounding result. As she scaled difficult parts of the rough road, Georgette would turn to see if the others were following, and it happened at one time that she noticed her mother close behind her, while a little lower down, Albert and her sister kissing each other. We should like to be able to say that this complete conjunction of four lips excited her indignation, but we should in that case be telling a falsehood. Georgette was much amused to note the state of fatigued security of her mamma, who took such trouble not to try and see what was going on behind her back. A thrill of mad gaiety ran through the young lass's frame, and she laughed so heartily that she was within an ace of tumbling down to the foot of the mountain. But the writhing brought on by her fit of merriment was the cause of a little accident in the interior of her well-nourished body, and twice the explosion of what poets have dubbed a sonnet, and what we call by a shorter word, as if one syllable of our chaste language was quite enough to designate this indiscreet detonation. At the sound of this trumpeting which was neither discreet nor modest, Madame Panat turned as white as her habit-shirt.

" Well, I never ! " she gasped, with a feeling of such consternation that it seemed she must have thought the rocky ground was slipping away from under her.

She was powerless to say another word. Georgette stopped dead, red and confused, and her embarrassment increased, as by the side of the indifferent guide, she saw Albert, looking slyly at her, a smile on his lips, and her sister glaring too. Henriette was green with fury, bad temper, indignation and perhaps shame. Georgette could not exactly divine what the grimacing physiognomy of her eldest sister portended, but she was sure it boded evil for her. She was very much troubled in every way.

The return home was sad and desolate, as lugubrious as the departure had been joyous.

In vain Albert tried a thousand times to rekindle conversation and create fresh merriment. He had to give himself question and answer, and took refuge in talking to the guide, who to lose his equanimity required something more than the sonorous, breezy breath of a feminine bottom. Henriette felt herself irrevocably dishonoured by this slight accident, and Madame Panat shared her disgrace. What would Albert think of such a breach of good manners; such impoliteness; an offence against the most elementary rules of civility? He would be bound to say to himself that these young ladies had received no proper care during their bringing-up, and he most certainly already suspected that Henriette allowed herself the same scandalous freedom as her sister. Who knows?—he might very likely think that they were cursed with some ridiculous infirmity. What would be the fate of the marriage after this? The fearful news would be spread about everywhere. Henriette would no longer dare to dine at the *table d'hôte*. They must hurry back post haste to Limoges, just at the moment when they had met this handsome, rich, clever, and amiable young man, whom Henriette loved, while he returned her affection, and was quite agreeable to make her his wife. He would naturally now hesitate at entering a family where the girls behaved in such deplorable fashion. He took no notice of his charmer, and chatted unceasingly with the guide. There was no doubt about it, he was greatly disgusted, and Henriette could understand his feelings.

" Oh ! the wretched, dirty little beast of

a girl!" she growled between her set teeth.

These sad thoughts so absorbed Henriette that she paid no heed to where she was going, and in a twinkling found herself in the midst of a thorny bush, causing her to utter a piercing cry. Albert turned round, caught her in his arms, so that she should no longer endure the pricking of the sharp briars, and tore her from their midst, but her thin muslin frock which she had put on despite her mother's advice to the contrary, got caught on a branch and torn from top to bottom.

Henriette was too dense to notice Albert's confusion, and supposed he had done this purposely and was the cause of her dress being well-nigh stripped off her back. She felt inclined to slap his face. She was a prey to rage and the greatest degree of shame, as she dragged the fragments of her dress at her heels, especially as not having anticipated this accident, she had that morning put on an old and common petticoat which was far from being immaculately clean.

"Oh! my poor child," asked Madame Panat, "what has happened to you?"

Luckily Albert had a few pins about him.

"You are our saviour," said Madame Panat, as kneeling behind her eldest girl, she took the pins one by one from his hand and tried to repair the disaster as well as possible.

Georgette, her hands on her hips, forgetting she was the cause of the misfortune, laughed like a pretty little angel of mischief and exchanged mocking glances with the guide.

"There! That's done! Now you can get along all right!" quoth Madame Panat to Henriette, who started off in a rage.

Gabas was reached once more in silence; the horses were put to, and after three hours, which seemed endless, they reached the Eaux-

Bonnes, in time for dinner. Henriette refused
to appear again at the *table d'hôte*, throwing herself in tears upon the bed as soon as she
reached the hotel. Her mother consoled her,
and tried to help her to feel fresh hope. Henriette wiped her eyes, determined to make
a final effort, and after taking a long time to
dress, she went down to the dining-room,
where trying to appear at her ease, she made a
sensational entrance. Wine and nice dishes,
with compliments from Albert who seemed just
as gallant as the day before, brought back all
her hardihood. She tried to be audacious
and grew too bold, saying a thousand artless
silly things that made everybody laugh at her.

As her neighbour asked her what was her
beau ideal among men, without listening to him
and thinking he was talking like some other
guests at the same moment about asparagus,
she replied :

" I like them when they are very big and long, with a fine violet knob that you can scarcely get into your mouth. And there should be lots of creamy sauce. "

Then she said also :

" Marriage changes a girl you know. My friend Louise used to be very quiet. Now she is much more open! " meaning that her young friend was less secretive and more frank than when single.

However, when she saw every head turned in her direction, and all eyes and ears fixed upon her lips, as she listened to the fits of gaiety each of her repartees caused to burst forth, she really believed, and so did her mamma, that she was meeting with great success. She was happy in her triumph, and got drunk with the outpouring of her own verbosity. But a too significant mocking glance of a neighbouring lady, and the long face pulled by Albert, revealed to her the true nature of the impression she produced.

" Why do you stare at me like that? " she said in a state of confusion, tears welling up in her eyes.

She imagined her adventure and that of her sister was known already, and that they were all jeering at her. Her assurance left her at once, and in her agitation, she knocked over a glass of claret which made a crimson stain on a young lady's white bodice. Without a word of excuse, she started up from the table. Her mother imitated her, and both women made good their retreat, with frowning brow, albeit sweeping along majestically, driving in front of them Georgette, who went off quite quietly, indifferent to the family catastrophe.

" The young one is very nice, but how rude her sister is! " was whispered as they passed.

Happily, neither Henriette nor Madame Panat heard this opinion, for they were so sensitive to worldly verdicts that they would have been in despair.

Henriette's grief changed into violent rage when she felt herself safe in the bosom of her family in her room, by her mother's side, in the presence of her younger sister, the cause of all her troubles.

" Didn't I tell you, ma, not to bring her with us?" she exclaimed.

" What's come over you now? Are you going mad?" retorted Georgette, who could not make out why her sister was so vexed with her.

Madame Panat quite agreed with her eldest daughter.

" Henriette is right. You behaved most ill-manneredly. You are responsible for all the misfortunes of the day! If Henriette misses this brilliant marriage, she owes it to you."

" To me? "

" Yes, to you alone.   Must I remind you of your filthy rudeness this afternoon?   You forgot yourself.   You committed the vilest indecency. "

" It was my shoe that creaked, " said Georgette, who remembered at last what she had done, and risked this lame excuse with a deep blush.

"You need not lie.   I heard you distinctly. "

" And so did I, " added Henriette.

" What then? " replied Georgette, trying another system of defence.   " It's impossible to restrain oneself now and again.   You the other day, at mass—"

" What do you mean, you little fool? "

" Are these the manners and politeness you've been taught at the convent?" said Madame Panat, without allowing Georgette to answer her sister.

" Oh! do let me be ! " cried the youngest girl at last, " you make me sick ! "

" Impertinent cat ! " cried Henriette, slapping Georgette's face with all her might, but the blow was no sooner received than she paid her sister back generously with two sounding smacks which metamorphosed the eldest girl's face into a tomato of the ruddiest hue.

" I forbid you to strike your sister ! " said Madame Panat, dragging Georgette away by the hair.

" She began ! " retorted Georgette using her hackneyed phrase in scenes of this kind.

"She has rights that you do not possess. She's older than you. You owe her obedience. "

Georgette's sole answer was a jet of saliva directed at Henriette's shoe, but she aimed badly and the spittle fell on one of her mother's boots. Never had the good lady experienced such a feeling of indignation.

" Do you know what you've done? " she enquired, her hand raised to strike.

" What I choose! " replied Georgette, shrugging her shoulders.

Madame Panat, her threatening fingers still uplifted, asked herself how she was to tame such an unruly daughter.   Henriette, her eyes full of tears of rage, came to her assistance.

" You are too soft-hearted, ma, " she said. " That girl will become a criminal, you'll see. She's allowed to do whatever she likes. "

" You must beg your sister's pardon on your knees at once. "

" Beg her pardon because she hit me? Never ! "

" This is too much !   Wait a bit and you'll see ! "

Madame Panat seized Georgette by the shoulders and tried to bend her down. But the young girl resisted with all her might and

main, kicking, biting, scratching. She too
was exasperated.

" Come and help me to punish her, Henriette, " said Madame Panat, breathless from
the effects of this struggle.

Mamma had no need to repeat her appeal,
and Henriette, throwing herself on her sister,
succeeded, despite her bucking, in holding her
down as Madame Panat desired.

" It's a shame ! " grumbled Georgette, her
head now under her mother's petticoats, gripped
between her fat thighs.

Unaccustomed to such an operation, Madame Panat was too clumsy ever to have succeeded if Henriette had not seconded her with
her help, and experience of cruelty. It was
she who lifted up her little sister's dress and
petticoat, rolling her chemise out of the way,
umbuttoning her drawers and dragging them
down to the garters. Madame Panat remained

impassible during this preparation, without
ordering or forbidding it.

" Mind you don't let your bottom speak up
again, you dirty beast. If you do, you'll have
an extra dose! " said Henriette.

" It's cowardly ! " groaned Georgette, in
cavernous tones, stifled between her mother's
legs.

" Will you have my belt, or the hearth
broom ? " kindly proposed Henriette.

" Let the broom alone. They'd put it in
the bill, " said Madame Panat, economical to
the last. " Pass me your waistband ! "

Madame Panat at first dealt rather light blows
on the budding buttocks, squeezed together
like shivering twin sisters afraid of a coming
storm, and resembling also an elegant Easter
egg, light and rosy; but when the hemispheres
were left free by subsequent distension, they
grew larger and appeared more vast, jutting out

impudently, full of pride and unrepentant; consequently deserving less clemency.   Madame Panat became implacable.   She struck at them with a vigorous hand, forcing loud groans from Georgette.

At one moment, the eldest sister, fearing that this chastisement might cause an open scandal in the hotel, went out into the passage to listen to the noise of the bottom-slapping.

" You can go on, ma, " she remarked, coming back in the room, and closing the door. " You can hardly hear a sound.   It's only as if you were dusting your clothes.   Your petticoats stifle her cries. "

Madame Panat seemed to take a fancy to this unwonted exercise. The peaceful, motherly woman, usually so calm, had gleams of furious vengeful joy in her little eyes, and she contemplated with lewd satisfaction akin to voluptuousness, the secret corrugated orifice in

the middle of the filial botto... stretched in pain
before her, and half open beneath her ferocious
cuts. The brown bottom-hole, no bigger than
a wee dot, tried to draw itself in and disappear
in the fleshy folds of the protecting posteriors,
but nothing saved it from growing more and
more scarlet every second under the barbarous
slashes of the belt. This indiscreet flower,
cause of all the harm, whose petals seemed so
many vibrating cords to propagate the burles-
que ringing blast and the comical music of
the intestines attracted her gaze persistently.

" There is the enemy of Henriette's
happiness," she said to herself. " There
lurks the venom that has poisoned her
life ! "

So as to approach the corolla more easily,
she pulled apart the meeting mountains of the
darling miniature bum, whilst the other hand
brandished the belt, the buckle swinging free and

unheeded, at the risk of seriously wounding the
victim.

" There !   Will that teach you to be decent ?
I'll show you what it means to break wind in
public ! "

All the barbarity and vileness that had
slumbered in her inmost being for years, at
the back of her husband's shop, awoke in a
second.

" Pity !   Pardon ! " implored wretched
Georgette.

Her mother, more out of fatigue than compassion, was about to throw aside the waist-belt,
when Henriette remarked :

" Look, ma, her left cheek is hardly red, "
and she spurred Madame Panat on to whip her
sister again.

At last, they left the sobbing lass to her shame,
lamentations, and suffering. Henriette, who
would have liked to prolong the whipping, went

away regretfully. She stood a moment in front
of the bleeding and broken skin of Georgette's
posteriors, as her young sister was lying on her
belly on the bed, not thinking, under the influence of excruciating pain, of covering up what
had been so liberally displayed.

" You can't say now that you haven't been
jolly well flogged, " said Henriette, her face
lit up with wicked joy, leaning over her
sister.

" Come, my dear child," said Madame Panat.
" Such a series of events, and all this emotion
has quite upset me. I want to take the air and
forget all about this sad day. "

" Where can we go, ma ? "

" To the theatre, at the Casino. We'll sit in
the back row of the stalls, if you don't care to
be seen. "

" With that little slut ? "

" Oh ! for goodness sake, no ! Let her stop

here, as a penance, and to prevent her gallivanting about, we'll lock her in. Come along, my dear girl. "

Madame Panat showed her eldest daughter out, and double-locked the door, leaving Georgette to sob at her ease.

Unfortunately for Madame Panat, but luckily for Georgette, old locks on hotel doors are not dependable.

The whipped girl had not noticed her mother and sister's departure at the moment, she was so overwhelmed with shame and confusion at having thus been flogged at her age in front of her sister. And in a hotel too, when the neighbours : a young man with mocking eyes, a tall lady with a disdainful nose, and all the children, so inquisitive and indiscreet, might have heard the blows. As all became silent at last, she sat up, and felt acute pain. It seemed to her now that some heavy load oppressed her,

and made her loins ache. She tried to get a
glimpse of her poor posterior, and stood up in
front of the mirrored wardrobe.   Madame Panat had flagellated Georgette's bottom methodi-
cally, without touching the thighs, whose white-
ness remained intact, while above the perfect
pair of columns, the living, vivid, throbbing
cupola appeared as if flaring with a mass of flames.
Her flesh was burning, and what frightened her
greatly was that as she touched herself in the most
secret spot of her frame, she felt her finger
growing moist, and found a little drop of blood
therein.   To calm the fiery heat devouring her
flesh, she went and fetched Henriette's vaseline
and powder, and after having thrown a pitying
glance at the bleeding reflection of her bare
person in the glass, she commenced smearing
the balm over her bruised bottom, when, lifting her eyes by chance, she caught sight of
three childish, saucy faces peeping at her with

amused and jeering astonishment. In the room where she was, there existed a door of communication, closed at present, but a piece of glass, very high up, above it, afforded a clear outlook from one chamber into the other. Two tiny girls and a little boy having heard a great noise in Georgette's bedchamber, had rigged up a regular scaffolding of tables and chairs so as to get a view of what was going on, and by the expression of their mischievous faces plainly gave signs that they felt inclined to see the show out.

These mouthing, jibing apparitions, joined to the mocking and indecent gestures they made behind the glass, so shamed poor Georgette that she hardly gave herself time to pull up her knickers and drop her skirts. She had but one idea—flight. The door that Madame Panat thought she had locked easily granted her an issue. But Georgette was no sooner in the

corridor, than she asked herself a question.
Where was she to go with her pot of vaseline?
The other rooms occupied by ladies stopping at
the hotel were all locked. She did not dare go
down to the drawing-room with her swollen,
red eyes. The water-closet was the only refuge left, but she could not decently spend the
whole of the evening there. She was in a
state of the most lively anxiety when a well-
known voice caused her to start fitfully.

" Halloa, mademoiselle ! Not at the Casino
this evening ? " asked Albert, owner of the
voice. " You seem to be in great trouble, "
he added.

Such words were exactly what were needed
to remind her of her misfortunes and intensify
them. Georgette began to sob as if in receipt
of fresh spanking. Just at that moment, the two
minxes and the saucy boy appeared at the end
of the corridor, escorted by their parents.

The whole family stared at Georgette with insolent curiosity. Her cup was full. Catching sight of an open and deserted room, Georgette dashed into it, so as to avoid her neighbours.

Albert followed and shut the door after him. It was his own bedchamber.

He drew the little girl on to the sofa, and invited her to confide in him, showing her every mark of interest and pity.

Choking sobs were at first the only reply he obtained. By dint of supplication, however, he succeeded in getting her to talk freely, and in accents, interrupted by pretty little moans, Georgette, with the genuine artless sincerity which such adventures would cause to arise in a young girl, told of her mother's plans; her sister's ambition; how Henriette imagined that she could make Albert's conquest; her vexation at the unsuccessful day's outing; and with what cruel injustice she had been made responsible for the great disappointment.

" But I don't love your sister at all ! " exclaimed Albert. " She is affected, artificial, and silly into the bargain. You're not a bit like her. Why should you be the cause of her awkwardness and embarrassment ? "

" She told me that my behaviour had put her out of countenance and you would be sure to think she was as badly brought up as I was. "

" It is she alone who is rude. "

" No, no. It is I ! "

" How do you mean ? "

" Didn't you hear—" faltered Georgette, looking uneasily at him.

" What ? "

" The nasty, dirty noise. I did it—with my creaking shoes. That is only what it was, I swear it. It's the truth ! I should never have dared—"

" Ha ! ha !" interrupted Albert, with a long laugh, lightly and lovingly slapping the guilty part of Georgette's young body. The blossoming buttocks, ignorant of their sin, spread themselves proudly out on the sofa, with all the more remarkable magnificence as Georgette, her elbows on her knees and her head leaning on her hand, drew in her bust. " Suppose even that you are telling a fib, is that such a great crime ? It is much worse to be false, scheming, and crafty like your sister. "

" Yet you made love to her, " Georgette ventured to whisper tenderly, as she heaved a sigh.

" I thought she was pretty, but I hadn't looked at you. I get quite angry when I think such a silly goose takes the liberty to lecture you. "

" She is always scolding me ! "

" Perhaps she did worse this evening ? "

Georgette's chin dropped and she did not venture to answer.

" But why were you walking about the corridor ? What have got hold of here ? A pot of vaseline ! "

She hardly dared confess, but at last she said :

" They nearly flayed me alive—ma and my sister—by flogging me. As I was spyed upon from the next room, I ran out in the passage. "

Despite the reserved nature of this explanation, Albert guessed the whole scene, and greatly pitied the victim.

" I'm a doctor, " said he—one lie calling up another—" and in my dressing-case I have some ointment which will calm the smart from which you are no doubt suffering, my little girl. Well then, lie down on my bed, and I'll anoint the painful parts. "

" I should never dare, " rejoined Georgette, blushing.

" Come, come, " said he, conducting her quickly.

He had very little trouble to make her recline face downwards, and in spite of the maiden's resistance, managed to pull up, one after the other, her skirts, petticoats, and chemise, which hid her ample charms.

" What adorable bum-cheeks! " said he. " What brute dared thus to bruise your tender skin? "

" Oh! monsieur, don't! " cried Georgette, frightened as she felt him untie her petticoat.

She was too tired, broken down by the long day's walk and the evening's emotions, and found herself unable to oppose any efficacious resistance to his endeavours.

It is extremely probable that Albert applied much balm to appease her pain, but he did not behave like a doctor. At any rate, not like an ordinary physician. In the midst of his nursing solicitude, his lips were not inactive, and doubtless after having applied his mouth to the still bleeding scratches as if to heal them, he did not refrain with bold practised skill from drawing down some fresh drops of vital fluid from the deepest and most secret part of her fleshly being. But he was so talented that there was no pain, and if Georgette experienced surprise and fury for a moment; if she found that he had taken advantage of her confidence and her sad plight; if she shed all the tears that remained to her while regretting the revelation and ravishment of the most precious part of her dear little body—cunning kisses, lively caresses, and passionate embraces made her forget her grief, initiating her to melting, unknown joys that stole away her senses. She fell asleep in Albert's arms, and enjoyed most delicious dreams in the bachelor's bed, if we may judge by the heavenly smile that accompanied her slumbers, and which her lover still cherishes in his memory as one of the greatest joys of his life.

What happened now, as a sequel to this adventure? Did Albert disappear without a storm, leaving Georgette to mourn her ingenuousness in silence? He would have been a fool and a rogue to have done so, for in mind, face, and fortune there were few young girls like his victim, and although she had shown him at their first meeting what others only expose after a long and troublesome courtship, she had more than one surprise and joy in store to grant to her husband. Moreover, had Albert so willed it, he could not escape from Madame Panat, who in a moment of temper was quite capable of slapping her daughter's bottom, but would never have abandoned her to what she called "dishonour." Georgette, returning to her room next morning, had to undergo the severe cross-examination of her mother and sister who had plainly seen that the young girl had not slept in her own bed. Georgette, trembling, begged that her sister should not be present while she confessed everything. Madame Panat consented, greatly to the indignation of her eldest daughter. Georgette, in low tones, with attitudes now timid, and then proud—for she had confidence in Albert's honourable intentions—made an incomplete avowal, but which sufficed to enlighten Madame Panat.

"Wretched child!" exclaimed the mother.

She went on to preach a long sermon, warning Georgette of the perils of her position, so infamous and shameful, in which she found herself through her vicious instincts.

But ma was not half as sorry as she seemed.

She too had faith in Albert. Georgette was very young, and although it would have been much more regular to marry the eldest first, still it was better to return to Limoges with a prospective bridegroom in tow, than not even to bring home, as she had feared at one time, the phantom of a man to divert her daughter's imagination, and satisfy her husband's paternal pride.

When Madame Panat saw Georgette crying, full of fear and confusion, she fancied that her discourse had produced a salutary effect, and putting on her darkest frock, smoothed her features until her face wore a most solemn expression. She had Albert's room pointed out to her, and entered at once with decided step, but without anger.

" I know what took place last night, " said she. " You most strangely misused my daughter, profiting by her youth and innocence. I could if I liked have you arrested like a vulgar malefactor. "

We shall not repeat all Madame Panat's speech, which was quite just and as befitted the occasion. We need only remark that Albert, a little tired after his arduous night, momentarily deprived by the very fact of his victory of all controversial spirit and warlike thoughts; intoxicated in short, by all the sweet memories Georgette had left in his brain, offered no defence. He declared that he was ready to repair all the harm that he said the grace and charm of the young girl was bound to drawn upon her.

" She is not a young girl, " exclaimed Madame Panat, " but a mere child! "

Albert gave information relating to his family, his property, and the influence of his family who if needed could obtain a dispensation, so as to allow Georgette to be married before the age of sixteen.

Madame Panat was good enough to be satisfied with his explanation and after a searching interrogating glance that penetrated to the lowest depths of her future son-in-law's soul, she shook his hand and retired.

The young husband's probation lasted several months, and the marriage was at last celebrated at Limoges with great pomp. Henriette feigned severe indisposition on her sister's wedding-day, so as to hide all the spite that devoured her.

Many months have passed since then and she has not yet found a partner for life.

Now hearken how history is written. People said that Henriette's clumsy rudeness had driven a rich betrothed suitor from her side; that a mountain guide, to be revenged on her for her coquetry and perhaps her infidelity, had, at the Eaux-Bonnes, bared the scraggy reverse cheeks of her body and slapped them until he drew blood, in presence of a vast crowd. To sum up, envious rumour ascribes to Henriette, with malicious exaggeration, all her sister's adventures and those which had such an unexpected *dénouement*.

As for Georgette, she keeps in the secret drawer of an old desk, the waistband by which her mother brought about momentary torture and the happiness of her whole life.

" If you only knew how we came to get married, " she often says to her girl friends, with a smiling side-glance at her husband.   " It was through such a trifling thing ! "

" No," he replies, " not insignificant at all ! "

And he cannot refrain from applying a little slap to the proud fleshy curves that spread out below his engaging wife's waist, and which beneath his impulsive caress, seem to expand and grow larger as if blooming more proudly than ever.

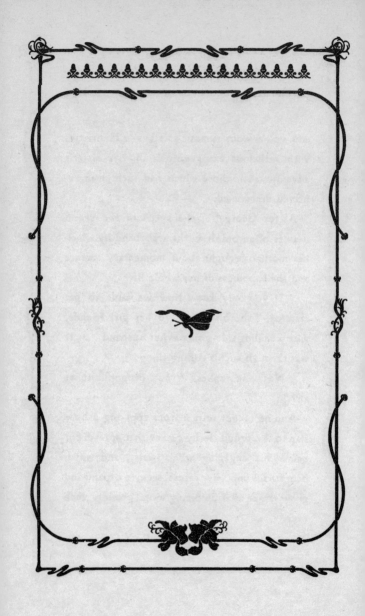

THE COLONEL AND

HIS COOK

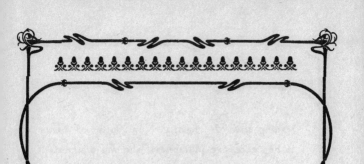

THE COLONEL AND
HIS COOK

Sidonie was a cook and possessed one of the most remarkable backsides in the world. She belonged to the race of wide-bottomed females, and truly had posteriors as big as those of three ordinary women rolled into one. When she stood erect she did not appear too stout, on account of her tall stature. Her eyes sparkled with malice and lust beneath her bushy brows, and there was something bold, self-willed, and energetical in her bearing. Her palpitating nostrils, thick red lips, and free gestures did not announce any pronounced leaning towards chastity. In spite of her rather excessive plumpness, she was a superb specimen of the maid of old-fashioned country inns, but she seemed rather out of place in the quiet villa of Colonel Montmauron. The lady's maid, Julie, also looked as if some other situation would have suited her better. She was a fat, fair young woman, with a stealthy look, who seemed as if she had just left some home of free love, vulgarly called a brothel. It was whispered that the general who at Nantes was at the head of the eleventh army corps, had kept them both as his concubines, and that after some serious scandal, his wife had promptly kicked out these creatures who shrieked and howled for extra wages. The general's lady had recommended the precious pair to her intimate friend, Madame de Montmauron, who felt herself in duty bound to take them in, if only on trial. During the

year she had utilised their services, Madame
de Montmauron had no great fault to find
with them. Indeed, she found that when she
was absent, they took good care of her two
daughters, little Marie; and the eldest girl,
Lucienne, who had just reached the age of
twelve. Being forced to go to Ireland, where
the colonel's wife possessed property and had
some relatives, she was therefore not too uneasy
at leaving her children behind. It seemed to
her that during the two or three months she
would have to be away, her husband, and the
cook and lady's maid would be able to take her
place and look after her little girls with proper
solicitude. She forgot that it was only her
cold and authoritative ways which kept these
servants in the path of duty, and that her
husband did not understand as she did, the art
of making himself obeyed and respected.

So the day after their mistress's departure,

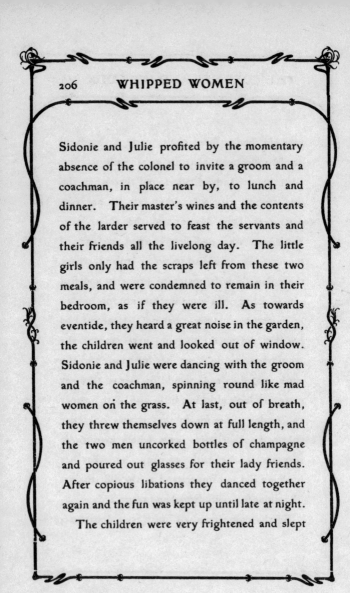

Sidonie and Julie profited by the momentary absence of the colonel to invite a groom and a coachman, in place near by, to lunch and dinner. Their master's wines and the contents of the larder served to feast the servants and their friends all the livelong day. The little girls only had the scraps left from these two meals, and were condemned to remain in their bedroom, as if they were ill. As towards eventide, they heard a great noise in the garden, the children went and looked out of window. Sidonie and Julie were dancing with the groom and the coachman, spinning round like mad women on the grass. At last, out of breath, they threw themselves down at full length, and the two men uncorked bottles of champagne and poured out glasses for their lady friends. After copious libations they danced together again and the fun was kept up until late at night.

The children were very frightened and slept

badly. The colonel never came home until
the next morning. One hour before his arrival,
Sidonie and Julie went and spoke to the young
girls.

" Have you ever been whipped? " the
serving-wenches said. " Oh! we mean a real
comfortable flogging, so that you can't sit
down for three days afterwards? No? Well,
you'll see how nice it is. You've only got to
tell your papa what you saw yesterday and
we'll let you have it at once, and tear all the
skin off your bottoms in a proper lady-like
way. You've only got to tell tales now—you're
warned! "

Marie and Lucienne, terrified by these
threats, took good care not to open their mouths
concerning the junketings of the preceding
day. But this did not prevent them being a
continual subject of apprehension for the
servants. The brace of sluts looked upon the

children like spies who were bound to denounce them, even unwittingly, some day or the other, so they undertook to get them out of the way. As they knew that the colonel's aunt always had her letters written by her lady companion, and was continually replacing her, Sidonie and Julie got up a false letter wherein the aunt asked her nephew in a most pressing way to bring his two daughters to stay with her in her country-house in the environs of Niort. Lucienne, who owed her aunt a grudge, because the old lady had whipped her severely during the last holidays, refused to go and visit her. So Marie went off alone with her father, and auntie was much surprised to hear that she had invited her niece, although she was well pleased to let her stop with her a month or two.

After a day's railway travelling, Colonel de Montmauron returned to Nantes rather late

at night, and reached his house in the Rue Saint
Clément. After having embraced Lucienne
who was fast asleep, he was about to retire to
rest, when he saw Sidonie in his bed.

His cook burst out in a great fit of laughter,
and then said familiarly :

" You didn't expect to find me here,
colonel? "

" It's perfectly certain that I could not fore-
see this. What does this stupid joke mean? "

" I thought that as your wife was away, you
might feel as if something were missing, and
without taking the liberty of thinking that I
can be a perfect substitute for Madame de
Montmauron, I beg to offer my consolation
all the same. "

" At this moment, " replied the colonel,
" I require less consolation than sleep. I'll
thank you to be kind enough to let me repose
in peace. "

" Are you made of stone? Look! Did you ever see bubbies like mine? "

Baring her bosom, she exposed her big breasts, where in the midst of each could be seen the enormous nipples, like two crushed strawberries. Then suddenly she rose up in bed, and kneeling with her face to the wall, her nightgown pulled up high, filling the room with her strong sexual odour, she offered in a magnificent lewd posture the vast rounded cheeks of her massive stern, divided into two equal hemispheres by a deep shaded dark line, where one could get a glimpse of a sort of fleshy and projecting rose, half hidden under black curls.

" You're a finely built woman, " said the colonel indifferently, winding up his watch, " but I must beg you to clear out. "

" Is that all you've got to say to me?" she replied, reclining on her side in a defiant attitude.

" That's all! I should not like my wife to know that I betrayed her—and with her cook too!"

" A cook indeed? Well, go and search among all your tarts and fine ladies, and see if you can find a girl better made than me!"

And Sidonie pressed her bosom and proudly slapped her backside.

" I told you you were well-built, " rejoined the colonel, " but that's not the question. If ever my wife got to know that I had been unfaithful, I should never forgive myself. "

" But she won't know! "

" These secrets always get found out. Then there's such a thing as decency. "

" You're a fool. If you won't let me sleep with you, then give me another bed. Mine is too narrow. There's no room for two in it. You've got a villa all to yourself, and you stuff your servant-girls into little children's rooms with dolls' beds in 'em. In this heat it's enough to choke a woman!"

"You can change your room. Take the one where the cupboards are."

"I ain't going to move in now, I suppose? Well, for to-night I find myself quite comfortable enough where I am, so here I sticks. That knocks you off your perch, eh? You can't put me in a dark cell, nor give me punishment drill, like you do to your men!"

"I'll go and fetch the police."

"I most certainly advise you do so, and everybody will be laughing at you to-morrow all round the neighbourhood, and over at the barracks."

The colonel was very vexed, as he walked up and down the room with tremendous strides, his arms crossed, asking himself what he had better do. Sidonie with mocking glances, watched him doing sentry-go, as she quietly rested on her side, throwing up her massive hip as if to give him a good view of what he affected to despise.

A few moments passed, and he had not made up his mind. Sidonie got out of bed, took off his hat and greatcoat, unlaced his boots, and forcing him to sit down, drew off his trousers. The colonel allowed himself to be undressed with more docility than a little boy.

" Now, *Monsieur*, to bed and quickly too! " she exclaimed; after having put him on his night-shirt.

She lit the hanging night-lamp, blew out the candles, and slipped between the sheets, close to her master who for the time being seemed to be her valet.

" For pity's sake, " he cried, " let me go to sleep! "

But Sidonie did not purpose letting him off

so easily. Her fingers wandered between her companion's hairy legs, and she hummed the fragment of a barrack-room ballad :

"Sweet soldier boy, grow up and get big,
Like the drum-major when in full fig!"

"You're a malingerer, that's what you are!" she suddenly exclaimed with a contemptuous shrug of the shoulders.

"In the Lord's name, I beg you to let me sleep!" sighed the colonel.

But his servant was too obstinate however to renounce her project so quickly. She dared to place the enormous latter end of her person close against her master's face, and when she had offered this contact, she ducked her head under the sheet, which she threw hastily back, as if searching in the bed for some lost jewel.

"Oh, gracious!" she exclaimed, after a few moments had passed, "I give you back to your wife. I see that you can await her return without suffering, but I pity the unlucky woman if she has only got you to amuse her. "

The colonel, with half closed eyes, and deaf to all she said, made a horrible grimace which took the place of a grateful smile.

" I am now confident, " he stammered in hoarse tones " that you are clever in all styles of cookery. "

" Am I? Then taste this, my boy! " she replied, becoming furious all at once, and as if to avenge herself, she forced an explosion, sounding noisily sonorous, as she blew in his face a series of breezy breaths which were a long way from being fragrant.

Next day, the soldiers were to march out of the town for musketry drill, and the colonel, who had left home early to go to the barracks, passed in front of his house at the head of his regiment.

Sidonie and the lady's maid, Julie, were on

the threshold, looking at the troops going by. They were impudent enough to make the coarsest remarks.

" Don't he look silly on his old crock? "

" What a guy! "

Then Sidonie improvised this irrespectful doggrel on the spur of the moment, adapting it to a popular tune :

> "When the colonel, half dead,
> Marches through the town,
> He can just hold up his head,
> But his sword hangs down!
> Down, derry down!"

The officers exchanged significant looks; some of the young chaps in the ranks could not refrain from laughing, but the colonel became as white as a ghost.

On returning home after drill, he said to Sidonie in tremulous tones :

" Why did you insult me before my men? "

" You insulted me worse last night! "

" You deserve to be kicked out of my house this very minute! "

" Do it, and I'll write to the missus at once. "

The colonel did not enjoy his dinner that evening. He seemed very uneasy, and the coffee had hardly been put on the table, when he said to the lady's maid :

" Tell Sidonie to go upstairs to my room. I want to speak to her. "

" Sidonie has just gone out, sir, " was the reply vouchsafed to him.

" Without my permission? This is too much of a good thing! "

But he was forced to swallow his rage. He went up to his bedroom which gave on the street, and waited at the open window, pricking up his ears at every noise, and trying to read until Sidonie should return. Hours passed; twelve o'clock struck, and the cook showed no signs of coming home.

About three o'clock in the morning, the colonel was just about to get into bed, when he heard someone at the servant's entrance, and ran down with all haste. Sidonie was there, out of breath, her hair hanging down and her attire in disorder.

" So these are your goings-on, my fine lady?   Slipping out without leave and coming home at daybreak? "

" What's the matter with him now? " said she, turning up her nose.

" I command you to come to my room at once! "

" Another time, old fellow.   To-day, I'm tired.   You can understand it and excuse me, for you were sufficiently dead beat yourself yesterday, if I don't mistake. "

Dumfounded at so much insolence, the colonel,

without another word or gesture, let her go up to her garret.

But all day she was polite and affable. Montauron did everything he could to sooth, coax, and court her, delighted to have an appointment granted him for the evening, for which he promised to remunerate her generously.

Why this sudden change? How was it that from being indifferent he had fallen in love? In reality it was his masculine vanity which threw him thus head over heels under his servant's skirts. He did not wish her to think he was such an old man, and was desirous of keeping up a reputation of virility. Moreover, the vile allurements, degrading but real; the will and pride that she showed, had all combined to conquer and subjugate him. He awaited her coming in his bedchamber, which was also that of his wife, with the keenest anxiety.

She made her appearance, and his desire,
and perchance also her skilful pandering tricks
made the couple forget the difference in their
ages. Sidonie pretended she felt tender affection.

" You ought to try and make your wife stop
away a bit longer, " said she. " How happy
we should be all the summer ! "

Her great idea, which she kept back for the
moment, as she did not quite feel she was truly
and completely the colonel's mistress as yet,
was to get rid of Lucienne as she had done with
little Marie. For this some specious pretext
was neccessary.

The connection of a maid-servant with a
child, little girl or boy, has something strange
about it. The infant is in closer contact with
its nurse than with the mother, because nearer
to animality. The wench is more familiar and
sometimes more indulgent than the parents,

and she enjoys her influence, often making bad use of it. It flatters her pride to humiliate her masters in their own flesh and blood. She likes to scold, sully, and strike the little ones confided to her care, even when she loves them, for then it is no longer the helpless infant she sees in them, but the offspring of beings she hates instinctively. In olden days this hatred was unknown, for the master was at the head of a family, of which the female servants formed part and parcel. He was both father and natural protector, and they could not help loving him.

Not only did Sidonie hate Lucienne because she was the future mistress of a household, but she felt innate repugnance. Such unreasoning dislike often arises between certain beings, as if they were representatives of naturally inimical races. Sidonie, a jovial, coarse brunette, could not stomach the graceful, fair girl, who was slightly affected and haughty, with the ways of a little woman, rather than those of a child.

The low and debased imagination of the queen of the kitchen was racked to invent means by which the little girl should become, momentarily at any rate, disagreeable or even odious in her father's eyes.

Lucienne being very clean and fond of looking and feeling tidy, Sidonie ingeniously tried to make her appear dirty. As Lucienne was in the habit of going to the privy before dinner, Sidonie dirtied the seat, and put out the light inside the water-closet. If Lucienne went afterwards to her washstand, she would not find a drop of water on it. And all this time Sidonie would make Julie hurry and call the child.

" Your pa is seated at table, waiting for you, *mademoiselle*. He's getting impatient. "

The scene may be imagined.

" Lucienne, how nasty you smell ! "

The young lass seemed quite dazed. At that juncture, the cook, who without sitting at table, now remained in the dining-room during nearly the whole duration of the repast, would draw Lucienne towards her, and kneel down behind her.

" Come here, and let me look at you. You're such a giddy little thing ! "

When her clothes were thrown up and her drawers pulled down, Lucienne revealed a chemise and posteriors which bore most infamous daubs and splashes.

" You disgusting creature ! " exclaimed the colonel. " You deserve to be birched. Sidonie, make her wash herself before you, and let her dine in her room as a punishment ! "

This mishap occured several times, always prepared by Sidonie, but she invented others which she thought would be more decisively

impressive, so as to humiliate Lucienne and
disgust her father.

One morning, when the colonel went to kiss
his daughter, Sidonie cut short all affectionate
effusions.

" Aren't you ashamed to be still in bed so
late?" she said to Lucienne, adding in authoritative tones : " Let me catch hold of your
fingers. "

At this, Lucienne slid her hand under
the sheets, but Sidonie dragged it brutally
forth, and smelt at the alleged guilty middle
digit.

" You've been touching yourself up again
this morning, you dirty little cat ! "

She then slapped her face twice or thrice
without the colonel intervening. Encouraged
by such mute approbation, Sidonie felt inclined
to be very severe.

" Turn your face to the wall !   Pull up your

nightgown and I'll give you a good slap-bottom!"

But the colonel showed some fatherly feeling, as he exclaimed:

"No, Sidonie, you shall spank her to-morrow, if she does it again. Let us be satisfied to-day to deprive her of her dessert. But to-morrow," he added, addressing himself to Lucienne, "I warn you that you'll not be let off so easily."

A week passed uneventfully. Sidonie could not manage to catch Lucienne napping, for her conduct was exemplary. The servant despaired of being able to get the young girl out of the house, when circumstances favoured her plans.

Some magnificent muscat grapes had been sent to the colonel, and he reserved them for a dinner he was giving that very evening in honour of several officers, his intimate friends. About six o'clock, Sidonie, who was laying the cloth, pretended to be looking for the fruit, and seeing Lucienne pass, she asked her :

" Have you eaten the grapes? "

" No, not I! "

" You liar! Who but you would do such a thing? "

" You perhaps, or somebody else! How should I know? "

Sidonie had just lifted her hand to smack Lucienne's face, when the colonel came upon the scene.

" What's all this? "

" If you please, sir, it's Lucienne who has eaten ten muscats, and says it's me! "

" What do you mean? My beautiful grapes! Will you answer at once, Lucienne? "

" I'll tell the truth, pa. I was tempted by the grapes, and I did eat a tiny little bunch. "

" Ah! ah! you are guilty then? "

" I only ate a wee cluster, five or six grapes

in all. Julie took the rest to the kitchen, and she and cook finished the lot. "

" You impudent, brazen thing ! " shouted Sidonie. " You must be longing for me to slap your bum by telling such a lie as that ! "

" Be quiet, Sidonie, " said the colonel. " Everything proves to me that the child is speaking truly. "

" Then I'm a liar ? Say I'm a liar at once ! "

" I don't know really ! "

" Answer me ! I order you to answer me ! "

" Go away ! You deafen and tire me, Sidonie. Leave the room ! "

" Not if I don't like ! "

She went, however, but passing through the hall, she turned round, and called out to the colonel :

" You can whistle for me all night if you like, but don't you think I shall come and rub up your wretched old toy for you ! "

" Sidonie ! " exclaimed her master, running after her, and catching hold of her backside.

" Let me be ! " she vociferated, " or I'll break wind in your hand ! "

" My Sidonie ! " he repeated beseechingly, not frightened at her threat. " Sidonie, promise to come to me to-night. Look, I'll give you this bank-note. "

" How much is it worth ? "

" Fifty francs. "

" Little enough ! Show it to me, anyhow, so that I may see if it's a real one. "

The colonel handed over the piece of blue paper, which she hurriedly glanced at and then stuffed it down her bosom. She turned towards him with a jeering grin.

" I meant to give it you to-night, " he said sheepishly.

" But I take it now. "

" You'll come all the same, won't you ? "

" That depends on you. I want you to say that I'm not a liar. "

" You're not a liar. "

" Yes, but you must repeat that in front of Lucienne, and tell her that she has calumniated me. "

" Oh dear! Oh dear! "

" That's not all. When you've said that, you'll have to scold her properly : ' For lying and falsely accusing your nurses, and having been greedy and a thief, you must go down on you knees and beg pardon of Julie and Sidonie, humbly asking them to to punish you by a good whipping.' "

" Oh, come now! What you ask is sheer madness! "

" Maybe, but you'll set about it immediately, or if not, you won't see me in your bed to-night. Better still—I'll be off with Julie and leave you in the lurch with your officers to get out of the mess as best you can. You can cook the dinner yourself, and serve it up how you like!"

"Sidonie, I pray you—"

"Are you going to obey me, or shall I leave the house?"

"At least, let me whip my child."

"No, you won't hit hard enough. You shall see us at work. It'll be much funnier for you!"

"You'll make me ill!"

"You—a soldier? You're not very courageous, old man. Look here, d'ye think we shall kill your gal? On the contrary, I'm sure you'll be amused, you fat swine, to see her bum-cheeks ruddled. You may rest assured it'll do her good."

"But my guests will soon be here!"

"Oh, we shan't be long about it!"

Thereupon she called Julie, who came up at once. Taking Lucienne, who had remained in the dining-room, by the hand, she led her into the pantry.

" You told a lie just now, *mademoiselle*, and I'll prove it to you. "

She felt quickly in the little girl's pockets, and then slipping her hand between Lucienne's pinafore and frock, pulled out a big bunch of grapes. Lucienne was quite as surprised as her father.

" Ha! ha! you daren't deny any more! Now, you little slanderer, you've got to beg both our pardons. Will you please speak to her? " she went on, nudging the colonel.

" Beg their pardon, Lucienne. "

" Never! "

" That's really one word too much! On your knees directly! Oh! I'll force you to kneel down. Julie, go and fetch the birch-rod! "

In vain did Lucienne struggle in Sidonie's strong arms. The cook shoved her hands under the child's clothes, and pulled her lace-trimmed knickers down to her heels, as she threw up petticoats and chemise together. Then, standing, she straddled backwards over the little girl's body, pressing her down with the full weight of her vast buttocks, forcing her to bend the upper part of her slight frame and jut out her posteriors.

" Help me to hold her! " said Sidonie.

" Julie will come and do that, " replied the colonel.

" Oh! papa! papa! " groaned Lucienne.

" You deserve what you're going to get, " mumbled the colonel, without conviction.

" Catch hold of her legs, " said Sidonie to the lady's maid, " and stop her kicking about, and struggling like this. "

Julie squatted down under Lucienne, placing the child's legs on her knees, holding them in her hard, horny hands, as if enchained.

Sidonie, her face leaning over the miniature, plump bottom, peered into the shadow of the dividing line, and pulling open the cheeks with her sharp finger-nails, she began talking in a vile way which drew forth the merriment of the lady's maid and made the colonel quiver with impatience.

" Look at this filth! Did you ever nose such a stink? A rag-picker keeps herself cleaner than you—little sow! Only let me catch you in this rotten state next time I pull down your drawers, that's all! I shan't whip you then. I'll flay the skin off your backside, see if I don't! "

" Come, be quick, and get this over, " reiterated the colonel.

" You, let me alone, d'ye hear? " retorted Sidonie.

At last, she seized the rod that the lady's maid had brought, and cut Lucienne's tender skin with its sharp points.   For the next few minutes, nothing was heard but one long, uninterrupted shriek.   Now and again the cry became a howl of rage, and Lucienne, in fury, tried, but unsuccessfully, to scratch and bite her tormentress from behind.   Sidonie often directed her strokes with all her might on the fissure between the ill-fated posteriors, which opened out; the twigs wounding and penetrating the little orifice.   The lady's maid was greatly interested in the contractions and swellings of the suffering bottom, which was a sorry sight, comical in spite of its misfortunes, framed between the two women's red and attentive faces, enlivened with the vilest and most ferocious joy.

" Come, I say, don't hit her in there! " said the colonel, as Sidonie pulled the buttocks apart.

" I'll teach her to be clean ! "

" But she's bleeding! She's had enough! "

" Let me alone! Hold her hands, that'll be more useful. She's preventing me thrashing her properly! "

A ring at the door-bell finally interrupted this odious chastisement, at which the colonel assisted in sorrow, but without daring to let his impudent mistress see how disgusted he felt. Lucienne went and threw herself on her bed, hiding her face in her hands.

" You haven't been birched at all, have you, dearie? You can't say now you don't know what a whipping is like! " said the lady's maid.

The little girl did not come down to dinner.

" My daughter is rather unwell, " said the colonel to his guests.

But as each course came on table, he served her share which Julie took upstairs at once.

After dinner, he went to see Lucienne, who was lying on her stomach, her head buried in the pillow, as if she did not dare to show her face. He took pity on her, and showed such commiseration that no one would have dreamed he was the cause of all her sufferings.

" My poor little girl! Are you still in pain? "

" Yes, very much. Ah! what you did was wrong, pa! "

" Come, come, you deserved it. "

" I didn't eat the grapes. "

" Oh, don't tell stories! I'll go and fetch you some cold-cream. That'll ease the smart of the birch. "

At midnight, the guests had gone. The colonel glided discreetly into his daughter's room. Lucienne slumbered heavily and uneasily, heaving little sighs which terminated in moans. He stood for a second, gazing at her.

" Poor child! " he gasped out.

Sidonie came upstairs, with nothing on but

a pink silk chemise, a gift from the colonel. She turned round to admire in the mirrors the sight of her backside thus draped, admiring the luminous folds that its large curves caused to glisten in the flimsy material.

" Sidonie, " said the colonel, " what you did was abominable. "

" So that's how you greet me, is it? All right, I'm off. But if I go, there's no danger that you ever see the end of my nose in your room again, my fine young fellow! "

" Don't get cross, Sidonie darling! "

" What's come over you now? Is your head dropping off? "

" Come in my room and let me explain matters. "

" I'll go with you on one condition, that you never allude to what has taken place this day. Your kid has been whipped for once in a way. She won't die of it. I got flogged so many

times that I can't count 'em.   It didn't prevent
me from enjoying good health and having
plenty firm flesh to sit upon, eh?   Now shut
up, or else talk about something else.   You
mayn't perhaps believe me, but I love you
to-night! "

She hustled him to the bed and rolled on it
with him.   Then turning round, and almost
stifling him under her mountains of flesh, she
inclined her head towards his feeble virile organ.
She rummaged until she found it, causing it to
wake from its lethargy and rise up.   By means
of her keen caresses and scientifically prolonged
kisses she brought about animation, and led it
to the goal of pleasure.   There was no resem-
blance between the colonel and the first Napo-
leon's generals, who albeit with snowy locks,
played the game of love and war simultaneously.   Sexual enjoyment coming thus on
top of the emotions of the evening, and a most

copious meal, washed down with champagne in galore and quite a reasonable series of little nips of brandy and liqueurs, had made him feel very sleepy. When Sidonie came and offered herself, she had a shrewd notion of the state he would be in, and expected to be able to profit by it. Without heeding her companion's yawns and drooping eyelids, she began thus :

" Just listen to me. Lucienne, as you recognise yourself, is becoming unbearable. We can't keep her here at home any longer; indeed, I shan't stop if she remains. The lady's maid will be off too. You'll never find a nurse for such a child. She requires constant watching— that you can see for yourself. Every morning she's so dark under the eyes that she looks as if she had been punched. She plays with herself all night, ruining her health. Julie and I have got our work to do. We can't be always at her heels. "

The servant continued in this way for some time, shaking the colonel now and again to prevent him dropping off to sleep.

" Why can't you listen to me? What I say is serious! " She summed up in these words : " There's only one thing left for you to do. Put her in the Ursuline convent, where she'll be well looked after. Speak up! You don't say a word?"

" I'll think over it, " said the colonel, stifling a yawn.

" There's no thinking wanted. You must make up your mind. Do it or leave it alone. If she don't leave the house, I shall, and so will the lady's maid. D'ye want me to go away?"

" You know I don't, Sidonie!"

" Well then," she rejoined, going and getting pen, ink, and paper, " put it down in black and white while I'm with you, so that you

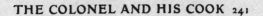

won't be able to say afterwards that you've changed your mind.

"'My dear Sidonie,'
"'I beg you to take Lucienne to-morrow to the Ursuline convent. You will arrange in my name with the Lady Superior about the price to be paid for taking a boarder during the holidays.'

" Good! Sign your name! Now, my boy, you'll see how happy we shall be without the kid who always had her eyes on us, preventing many a nice kiss. First and foremost, we shall be able to dine together, like a little pair of real lovers, and Julie, who is a jolly and a pretty girl, will join us. It'll be gayer than having to sit in front of that stupid little slut, with her dirty unwiped bottom. Come now, don't get cross! You don't even know if she's your daughter or not!"

She would have kept on talking much longer, if she had not perceived by the sudden thunder of his snoring, that the colonel was fast asleep. She carefully folded the letter, after adding the date; pinned it to her chemise, and stretched herself quietly by the side of her master, who had become her trembling lackey, entirely subservient to her slightest whim.

Next morning, the colonel rose in a good humour, embraced Lucienne while she was in bed, lunched out, and stopped away all day, without recollecting what he had written the night before, when half asleep. Accordingly, he was greatly astonished at dinner-time not to see his daughter.

" Is she ill ? "

" No, of course not, " replied Sidonie. " I took her to the convent this afternoon. "

" What convent ? "

" Didn't you tell me you wanted to confide her to the care of the Ursuline sisters while your wife was absent ? "

" Did I say that? "

" You did more—you wrote it. Look at this letter. Can't you recognise your own handwriting? "

" I must have been mad. You've imagined this scheme to rid yourself of my child. You detested her! But she shan't remain in a convent, damme! I'll not have it! You must fetch her out this very evening and bring her home. "

" Impossible! You'll not be able to see her until Thursday—the next half-holiday. "

The colonel burst into a fit of temper, smashed a few plates, and broke a chair, but the noisier were his furious attacks, the less time they lasted. Sidonie let the storm fizzle out, and then recommenced her argument of the preceding evening. The girl was in need of constant watching. Convent life would profit her. Would they not be much happier alone,

without having someone in front of them spying on their caresses?

Sidonie finally coaxed and won the colonel over, so they had a very merry dinner.

For the first time, Sidonie sat at her master's table on equal terms. But no, she was now sole mistress. It was a loving repast, where kisses caused the imperfect cooking and attendance to remain unheeded. Not one dish was properly served, and as Sidonie had invited the lady's maid to dine with them, each of the three in turn got up to fetch clean plates and whatever else was required.

That night a travelling company appeared at the theatre. In vain the colonel made all sorts of excuses for stopping at home.

" Yes, yes, " begged the two women, " let us all three go together ! "

" But my brother officers and the general himself will be there. It'll look awful ! "

" Then you're ashamed of me ? " vociferated Sidonie.

" Not a bit of it, but—"

" There's no ' but ' about it. You must take us. Without boasting, we're better looking than your general's wife—stuck-up old thing !—and all your officers' jades. I know 'em ! There's not one among the lot fit to be my maid-of-all-work ! "

The colonel still tried to resist, but at last he gave way to the prayers of the two women. They even wanted him to put on his uniform and it was not without a deal of trouble that he got Sidonie to grant him permission to go in mufti.

As for the wenches, despite their good looks, like all women, they were only enticing in their habitual dress. Pleasing enough in servants' frocks, they became ridiculous in their best clothes. So they were hardly seated in a private box on the ground tier, that the colonel paid for, than mutterings and scarcely polite remarks were heard in the stalls. Sidonie, her clenched fists on her hips, like a fish-fag, rose and shouted at her critics with her insolent voice which resounded all over the auditorium. Cries of " Turn her out ! " were already uttered, and it looked as if the police were about to interfere, when the curtain drew up, and Sidonie, forgetting her fury, sat down again, flushed and gasping for breath.

" It's a most amusing play, " said Sidonie, as the act-drop fell at the close of the first tableau.

" I've just caught sight of the general, " replied the colonel. " He can see us from his box. "

Fearing, if he left his seat accompanied by the two women, to be met by some of the officers ; while at the same time, if he remained

with them during the entr'acte there might be
a quarrel between his servants and the specta-
tors who continued to make fun of the girls'
eccentric get-up and the false jewellery with
which Sidonie was covered, he asked them if
they would like some refreshment, and on
receiving a reply in the affirmative, he
gave them a louis to go and have some
champagne.

" Aren't you coming with us, dear ? "

" Oh no ! " he exclaimed, hiding himself at
the back of the box.

The curtain had been up over a quarter of an
hour when they returned chattering together.
This time they paid but little attention to the
play, but conversed in whispers, glancing now
and then at the colonel as if alarmed lest he
should overhear what they said, but he was too
far behind, and too much taken up with the
care of trying to remain unseen by the general

to listen to their talk, which was in low tones, carried on with their mouths close to each other's ears.

During the second interval, he made them go off for a walk again. He would have liked to have sent them to the devil that night, and sunk himself into the earth so as not to be caught by the general. At any rate, his women left him in peace during the remainder of the entertainment, for they did not deign to reappear during the third, fourth, or fifth acts. He felt very uneasy and humiliated when he left the building, still looking about for them and unable to realize that they should thus have abandoned him.

" Where are they ? Where can they be ? " he kept on repeating.

He hoped to find them at home when he reached his house, but they were not there.

When he went up to his bedroom, he found

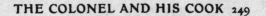
his desk open. He quickly rummaged in a drawer where the day before he had put six thousand francs. The money was gone.

A sealed letter had been placed on the middle of the table so that it could not remain unperceived. He opened it. It was from Sidonie, and this is what it said :

"My dear friend,

"As you don't seem to understand what courage is required to amuse a limp old dotard like yourself, I'm off! I've had enough of you! You must admit that if a cook has to be paid, the peculiar kind of service I've rendered you deserves much higher wages. You're not one of the generous sort —that I've known for some time past, worse luck! But I don't intend to suffer through your stinginess, and I've helped myself.

"If this style of giving my demission don't please you, you can say so. But first of all, just think over what I'm going to say. I've sneaked out of the house of your friend Riviere some letters you wrote to him last year, where you speak quite freely about the general, the Minister of War, and the government.

"These notes will be useful if you want to gain higher rank in the army, that's certain, and I shall not fail to send them to some people you know, which I am sure will please you vastly.

"If you should be going to the Ursuline convent, you won't find your daughter. That's a sure thing, because she isn't there. If you want to see her and have her home again, you must hand over four thousand francs to the man who'll call upon you the day after to-morrow. If anything disagreeable should happen to me or the person I shall send, you know what to expect: your letters to Riviere will be sent to the right quarter, and you'll never set eyes on your little daughter again.

"I hope to hear from you very soon.

"SIDONIE."

" What a monster ! " exclaimed the colonel, who could never have imagined that such perfidy existed.

He asked himself in fright what he should do. He always trembled in front of his wife, as he had trembled before his cook-concubine, and knew not how he could explain the disappearance of these ten thousand francs when his better-half should come home. She would certainly have suspicions, and leave him, a contingency he feared the more because all the money came from his wife. Nevertheless he was longing to see his poor little Lucienne again.

Suppose this vile woman should keep her a prisoner somewhere and do her harm? She was quite capable of such a thing. And how about the letters containing such free comments on the doings of his superiors and the members of the government? What would be said about it if they fell into the hands of the Minister of War? The colonel might be dismissed the army.

Thus worried, he strode up and down his room, continually repeating :

" What an abominable creature ! Oh, what a monstrous female ! "

Instead of conducting Lucienne to the convent, Sidonie had taken her in a hired vehicle to a most dirty little hotel in a small back street, at the other end of the town. When they alighted, all the lodgers—women with their hair hanging down and drunken sailors—were lolling out of window.

" Where are you taking me ? Whither are you leading me ? " were Lucienne's unceasing questions.

" Hold you jaw! I'm not bound to answer you," replied Sidonie, when it pleased her to open her lips. " If you bother me, I'll whip you like I did yesterday."

She made a sign to an old woman in the office of the hotel, and a key was handed to her. She clambered to the top of a staircase as narrow as a ladder, dragging up the little girl who was much alarmed at the jokes of the seafaring men and the half naked women she saw appear on each landing, coming out of rooms where everything was in disorder.

In this way, they reached a little attic. Sidonie locked the door, and said to Lucienne :

" Strip at once! "

As Lucienne, quaking with fear, hesitated about obeying, the cook unbuttoned her little jacket and dragged it away. She then successively took off her skirt, petticoat, chemise, drawers, and even her shoes and stockings.

The little girl seemed greatly affrighted as she stood stark naked, her arms crossed on her breast. Sidonie, however, was amused at the sight of the girlish, shuddering, fair-skinned frame, where all was smooth and white, save the buttocks which still showed traces of the biting birch.

" What did you think of my rubbing-down yesterday? " asked Sidonie, with a demoniacal grin, as she lightly smacked the young backside which seemed to inspire her brain with cruel cravings. " Aha! it didn't give you pleasure, eh? You'll have plenty more birchings, I warrant you, what with your rotten disposition and your obstinate head. You ain't out of the wood yet, my gal! "

So saying, she opened a cupboard, and drew forth a complete young village lass's dress : skirt, bodice, woollen stockings, a chemise of thick brown calico, a starched local headdress, as worn by a peasantess of Nantes, and hobnailed shoes.

At first Lucienne was thunderstruck, and then began to cry when Sidonie ordered her to put on this attire. But the cook paid no heed to her lamentations. She dressed her by main force, slapping her bottom at intervals when Lucienne revolted against such a strange style of costume.

When she was thus disguised, Sidonie took her downstairs again and forced her into the *fiacre*, once more. They got out soon afterwards in a street near the railway station. A tall, rather stout female, dressed like a country woman in a cap, with the eyes of a bird of prey and sensual nostrils, was standing at the door of a tavern.

" Ah ! there you are at last ! " she said, smiling sardonically.

" I give the kid over to you, Madame Plouvier, and think she'll suit. Only she's got a mania that comes out now and then: she fancies she's some fine young lady. You musn't put up with that. When you have had her backside bare five or six times, she'll grow out of it. "

" She ain't too bad-looking, " said Madame Plouvier.

" I should think not indeed! Come on, give us what you promised. And hurry up, because the train starts in a few minutes. You're only just in time. "

Madame Plouvier dropped two gold pieces slowly, as if regretfully, into Sidonie's palm, and bustled off to the station, followed by Lucienne, who, terrified, seemingly annihilated by the cook's threats, abandoned herself to Madame Plouvier.

" Good bye, my little gal ! " shouted Sidonie. " Enjoy yourself ! Mind how you behave, or you'll catch it ! "

And she made the gesture of slapping the back of her left hand with the fingers of her right.

Madame Plouvier and Lucienne got into a third-class compartment full of people, just as the train was leaving the platform. There was only one seat left, and Madame Plouvier took it. Lucienne had to sit on the floor at the feet of her new guide. At each station she was hustled and trod on by travellers going out or coming in. But soon she seemed heedless of kicks and cuffs, the movement of the train nursing her into slumber.

At dark, the woman and the colonel's daughter left the train and took the diligence which passed through thick woods and followed steep roads. The coach, driven at a high rate of speed, rolled every instant from side to side as if about to fall over. It struck Lucienne that she was being plunged into some barbarous and unknown land. She was sore afraid, but held her tongue, and never stirred. It was bright moonlight when they arrived in a little village consisting of some twenty houses. The horses pulled up in front of a door surmounted by a green board, on which could be read in white letters : " Plouvier, Grocery. " Madame Plouvier told Lucienne to get down.

" Come on ! " cried the woman. " Make yourself useful once in your life ! "

She passed her down a lot of baskets and enormous bundles. The poor child gave way beneath their weight and nearly fell down.

However, this was the end of her misery for that day at least. After having swallowed a bowl of soup, she undressed herself almost mechanically, and without looking where she was, tumbled in a heap on a bed that was pointed out to her, and fell fast asleep at once.

" Hurry up! You've been lazy quite long enough! " was shrieked at her in acid tones early the next morning, while drops of cold water were dashed in her face.

Lucienne woke with a start, surprised at finding herself in the middle of a whitewashed room with a low ceiling. Facing her stood a stout woman, the picture of her travelling companion, who pulled off the sheet of the narrow bed whereon Lucienne had passed the night, and made her hasten to get up. Lucienne dressed with lightning speed, and without being allowed time to wash herself, had to go down into the little grocer's shop where she found Madame Plouvier herself.

" Justine, " said the latter, " show the girl what she has to do. I must go to the fair to-morrow and you two will have to manage all the work between you. "

Justine was the younger sister of Madame

Plouvier, who ordered her about like a servant, but Justine did what she chose and always had her own way.

She told Lucienne to sweep and dust the shop, making her do what she was told several times over, for she was never satisfied. Then Lucienne had to serve the customers, and it was all she could do to move and replace barrels, glass jars, and the heavy boxes she was ordered to bring forward. But all this was so novel for her and she had so little time allowed her for reflection that she applied herself ardently to her task as if playing some new game. She even enjoyed with a good appetite a bowl of wretched broth with black bread which was given her, and all passed off tolerably well during this first day.

Next morning, things changed. At six o'clock she was awakened by several blows given her with a broom.

" Did you think I should let you play the sluggard long? " shouted Justine.

The two sisters had made up their minds not to spare her. She received innumerable boxes on the ears and kicks. But it was only two or three days later that she got her first slap-bottom, having been caught filching some of the jam destined to be sold to customers. Justine took her in the back-shop and put her head between her thighs, under her dirty petticoats. Having pulled up the wretched girl's clothes, she brutally spanked her posteriors with the sole of her slipper. After this thrashing, Lucienne dared not lift her eyes. But there was worse punishment and humiliation in store, when she broke a bottle of liqueur. They bound her to a wooden bench by her hands and feet, for fear she resisted or kicked, and thrashed her with thick ropes. As she bit Justine, they tore her tender skin with frightful cuts of bunches of furze, and caned her besides.

Madame Plouvier often helped her sister to hold Lucienne, or to whip her. She made but two objections to these chastisements.

" Don't expose her backside in the shop. You may disgust the customers. "

" On the contrary, it amuses them. "

" You'll wear out all my brooms. Aren't there birches enough? Haven't you got a martinet? "

" I flog her buttocks with what comes first to hand! " replied Justine.

The worst torture of all for Lucienne was public correction in the open shop, in the doorway, or in the garden behind the grocery; and these flagellations were frequent. She might have managed to escape them, for she always got whipped for the same motive : pilfering in the shop. But she was so badly fed, that it was not astonishing she could not resist eating or nibbling the nice things she found around her: raisins, prunes, almonds. Little robberies which remained undiscovered encouraged her to more important pillage, and when she was left alone for a second, she tried to capture some fruit, a small cheese, or a pot of jam, but she was nearly always caught red-handed by Justine, who would rush at her precipitately.

" Ah ! greedy little pig ! Thief that you are ! Your bum shall pay for your belly, see if it shan't ! "

Lucienne struggled, and asked to be pardoned, but Justine, unheeding her, dragged her to the corner where stood her broom or birch, for she varied her mode of punishment. Sometimes women came in to make purchases and assisted at the execution, chatting with Justine, or even lending a hand.

" If you're too busy thrashing your apprentice, we'll come back some other time. "

" No, no, my sister will serve you. "

" Oh ! I can wait, " said one woman, taking a seat ; and turning towards a female who accompanied her, she added : " It'll be a good lesson for you, Madame, to see how young minxes should be tamed. You've got a big growing girl of your own. I hear she's not always easy to get on with and that you are too timid to lay a finger on her. "

" What nonsense ! I gave her a good spanking this very morning. "

" Excuse me, ladies, " said Justine, " my sister is out. Will you be so good as to wait a few minutes while I whip my servant ? I think a good flogging should never be postponed. It loses its effect. "

" You're right. When a child has misbehaved, the penalty ought to be paid at once.

Oh ! how she wriggles !   Shall I hold her for you ? "

" Thanks.   Now she's tamed.   When I've got her like this, under my arm, head downwards, I don't need any assistance to give her her due. "

Justine, just like Sidonie, found the same delight in vilely humiliating Lucienne, by her preparations, remarks, and examinations of her body.

" I beg your pardon, ladies, but I'm forced to expose her wicked stern.   I like to see what I'm about. "

" So do I.   There's nothing so deceiving as those bothering petticoats.   You think you've finely flogged the slut and all the time you've only been knocking the dust out of her rags. "

Despite her kicks and bounds, Lucienne was powerless to prevent her one petticoat being pulled up, and her fleshy, plump backside, thus forced to jut out, appeared in all its ample, girlish glory.

" What a grand target ! " remarked one of the lady customers. " If the little bitch gets a bit above herself, there's something to hit at anyway ! "

Justine paused as she fixed her eyes attentively on some spots she noticed on the chemise, and she pulled Lucienne's buttocks apart.

" Oh ! the dirty wretch ! Disgusting creature ! " she cried. " I'll teach you to show a clean bum when I whip you. " She thrust one of her big fingers in the indecent secret aperture. " I always take this precaution with unwiped little girls. When their guts are full and they get the stick, the vile sluts are capable of letting go all over you ! "

At last she lifted her broom, and directing her blows at the fissure between the two pretty globes, her cruelty caused Lucienne to howl in pain.

" You've sinned through your mouth ; you must suffer by the lower lips, " she shrieked. " Ah ! I'll give you something to eat ! "

Pulling the little girl's backside open with one hand, she never ceased swishing the mysterious brown button-hole. Lucienne lost her voice, so loudly did she cry out, supplicate, beg for forgiveness, and insult the whipping harpy. A purple band, surmounted by a kind of bleeding eyelet-hole, could be seen in the middle of the large disc, which was scarcely flushed with pink marks, having been spared so far.

The two witnesses bent over the victim, not afraid of receiving right in their faces the malodorous sighs that her posture, rage, pain, and forgetfulness of herself drew from Lucienne's hinder parts.

" I've got my own ways of pickling their backsides, " said Justine. " When I've done with the dirty drabs, they can go and sit on the privy as much as they like, I guarantee they don't think of messing themselves about. "

The grocer-woman ceasing her correction for a moment, Lucienne tried to stand up, but Justine never loosed her hold.

" Wait a bit, " said Justine, " I ain't done yet. "

She furiously attacked the surface of the buttocks which became of a violet-red hue, and drops of blood spurted out.

The broom was worn to a stump, and Justine had beaten the child with such ardour, experiencing such cruel intoxication, that she was tired out.

" Now then ! Get up ! " she exclaimed.

" She won't lose what you've given her however fast she runs, " remarked one of the custo-

mers pointing to Lucienne, who with her face
in her hands, choking with sobs, and her skirts
still half up, fled to the end of the garden.

" Come here, I tell you! " ferocious Justine called after her. " I didn't whip you to
make you howl and grow lazy. Come and
serve these ladies, or I'll begin all over again! "

Lucienne had to show her face flushed with
shame, and her eyes full of tears, as she fetched
boxes of biscuits, tins of preserved vegetables,
or dried fruits. She had to go up a ladder,
and be bustling and active, while scarcely able
to stifle a sob or cry of pain at each movement
she made. She could not refrain also from
placing her hands on her poor smarting bum-
cheeks.

Lucienne would have liked to write to her
father, but she never had a moment to herself.

She had always to be in the shop, and Justine and her sister so tyrannised over her that

if by chance she was alone with a customer who asked her any question, she did not dare to reply.

One day, when she happened to drop a glass jar, smashing it to atoms, Justine pursued her to the market-place with her broom, and catching her at last, she dragged her home, slapping her face all the way, and driving her knees into her backside to make her get along faster. When she reached the door of the shop, either because she could no longer control her rage, or wishing to humiliate Lucienne still more by a punishment in public among all the passers-by, she forced her to kneel in the doorway. There she pulled up her clothes, and started flogging her with her habitual cruelty. The villagers turned to look at the young girl's behind, and enjoyed the sight of the globes gradually reddening beneath the shower of blows. But an old lady, wearing

corkscrew curls and a large gipsy bonnet, stopped suddenly, and throwing her arms up in
the air, exclaimed :

" It's shameful to beat a child like that ! "

" Mind your own business, " replied Justine, without ceasing her fustigation.

The old lady's remark recruited a few parti-
sans. Several persons declared that children
ought to be corrected but not martyrized. Justine did not wish to increase the general growing
dissatisfaction.

" I'll spank you to-night in the water-closet,
dirty little beast ! " she whispered in Lucienne's
ear. " Like that, nobody will hear you ! "

She dropped the broom and let Lucienne
howl at her ease. After having sobbed a
moment, the little girl got up and ran away
from the grocery.

" Great heaven ! 'Tis Lucienne ! " exclaimed
the old lady, rushing towards her and

taking her in her arms. " Lucienne, my dear
little girl ! " she said, as she kissed her. "Don't
you know your poor old aunt ? "

The miserable damsel lifted her eyes swim-
ming with big tears and uttered a cry of glad
surprise.

" Aunt Léontine ! "

Aunt Léontine lived in the country all the
year round, and had not been to town to see
her nieces for over two years. That is why
Sidonie did not know her, and was entirely
ignorant of the fact that Aunt Léontine lived
in the identical village where she had sent the
colonel's daughter.

When kind caresses had somewhat calmed
Lucienne's grief, Aunt Léontine wanted to
know how it was that her niece had come to be
in the grocer's shop. She was astounded at
the child's story.

" It's extraordinary ! " she kept on repeating, and continuing, she said : " Come with me ! "

Lucienne was seized with fresh fright when she saw her aunt taking her back to the grocery.

" Don't be frightened in the least, " the old lady said to her, " you'll not stop there long. "

She had hardly entered the shop when she adressed herself to Justine :

" Are you not ashamed thus to torture a defenceless infant ? "

" I slap her bottom when she deserves it, " replied Justine, " and unfortunately she often merits a spanking. "

" You are a wicked woman, " said Aunt Léontine, " and I shall take the girl away from you. "

" Begging your pardon, " shouted the shopkeeper, " I've paid the girl's mother, or stepmother, a year's wages in advance. "

" How much was that ? "

" Forty francs. Then there's the railway journey. "

Aunt Léontine opened her purse, took out three gold pieces, and threw them on the counter.

" Now, let's be off ! " said auntie.

After having examined the louis one by one, Justine turned towards the aunt who with her niece had already crossed the threshold.

" Good bye and good luck to you, old lady, but you'll not do much good with the little trollop by spoiling her. At my place, with many a good slap-bottom, she would have blossomed into a useful servant girl ! "

Aunt Léontine wrote at once to the colonel who arrived two days afterwards, and was so overjoyed at finding his daughter once more that he did not think of avenging the affronts she had received.

In the meanwhile, Sidonie had been warned.

Vexed at not being able to blackmail the colonel, she tried to do him all the harm she could. The compromising letters were made public, and anonymous notes sent to the colonel's wife, where her husband's infidelity was fully revealed.

M. de Montmauron was too weak and timid to defend himself and put a bold face on the matter. He thought his wife would never forgive him, and that he could no longer remain in the army. He sent in his demission, and started secretly for Paris with his daughter Lucienne who was very much attached to him. He lived in poverty, and Lucienne, grown to womanhood, was forced to offer her charms to the first passer-by, for want of a crust of bread. Despite her girlish grace and beauty, she was still obliged, when we made her acquaintance, to go out each night to public halls and concerts, searching for a gold piece to pay for the next day's food.

Sidonie, fearing prosecution, took to the best hiding-place she knew of—a brothel. It was there that the Count de la Roche-Thiaudière found her. He was quite a young man, but rather weak-minded, and fell under the charm of the shamelessly lewd caresses of the former cook. He made her his mistress, and then married her. She treated him worse than the colonel, like a slave, boxing his ears in public, and going further when there were no indiscretions to be feared. She betrayed him afterwards if he dared to take umbrage at her caprices.

Victim of this vile accouplement, the wretched man's strength failed him, and his health was ruined. He fell into a decline and finally died. At present, Sidonie is Countess de la Roche-Thiaudière. She possesses one of the finest fortunes and grandest estates in the whole of France.

THE END

Available now

The Captive
by Anonymous

When a wealthy Enlish man-about-town attempts to make advances to the beautiful twenty-year-old debutante Caroline Martin, she haughtily repels him. As revenge, he pays a white-slavery ring £30,000 to have Caroline abducted and spirited away to the remote Atlas Mountains of Morocco. There the mistress of the ring and her sinister assistant Jason begin Caroline's education—an abduction designed to break her will and prepare her for her mentor.

Available now

Captive II
by Richard Manton

Following the best-selling novel, *The Captive*, this sequel is set among the subtropical provinces of Cheluna, where white slavery remains an institution to this day. Brigid, with her dancing girl figure and sweeping tresses of red hair, has caused the prosecution of a rich admirer. As retribution, he employs the underground organization Rio 9 to abduct and transport her to Cambina Alta Plantation. Naked and bound before the Sadism of Col. Manrique and the perversities of the Comte de Zantra, Brigid endures an education in submission. Her training continues until she is ready to be the slave of the man who has chosen her.

Available now

Captive III: The Perfumed Trap
by Anonymous

The story of slavery and passionate training described first-hand in the spirited correspondence of two wealthy cousins, Alec and Miriam. The power wielded by them over the girls who cross their paths leads them beyond Cheluna to the remote settlement of Cambina Alta and a life of plantation discipline. On the way, Alec's passion for Julie, a golden-haired nymph, is rivaled by Miriam's disciplinary zeal for Jenny, a rebellious young woman under correction at a police barracks.

Forthcoming

Captive IV: The Eyes Behind the Mask
by Anonymous

The Captives of Cheluna feel a dread fascination for the boy whose duty it is to chastise. This narrative follows a masked apprentice who obeys his master's orders without pity or restraint. Emma Smith's birching would cause a reform school scandal. Secret additions to the frenzy of nineteen-year-old Karen and Noreen mingle the boy's fierce passion with lascivious punishment. Mature young women like Jenny Woodward pay dearly for defying their master, whose masked servant also prints the marks of slavery on Lesley Hollingsworth, following *Captive II*. The untrained and the self-assured alike learn to shiver, as they lie waiting, under the caress of the eyes behind the mask.

————

Available now

Captive V: The Soundproof Dream
by Richard Manton

Beauty lies in bondage everywhere in the tropical island of Cheluna. Joanne, a 19-year old rebel, is sent to detention on Krater Island where obedience and discipline occupy the secret hours of night. Like the dark beauty Shirley Wood and blond shopgirl Maggie Turnbull, Jo is subjected to unending punishment. When her Krater Island training is complete, Jo's fate is Metron, the palace home of the strange Colonel Mantrique.

Available now

SHADOW LANE

In a small New England village, four spirited young women explore the romance of discipline with their lovers. Laura's husband is handsome but terribly strict, leaving her no choice but to rebel. Damaris is a very bad girl until detective Flagg takes her in hand. Susan simultaneously begins her freshman year at college and her odyssey in the scene with two charming older men. Marguerite can't decide whether to remain dreamily submissive or become a goddess.

———

Available now

SHADOW LANE II
Return to Random Point

All Susan Ross ever wanted was a handsome and masterful lover who would turn her over his knee now and then without trying to control her life. She ends up with three of them in this second installment of the ongoing chronicle of romantic discipline, set in a village on Cape Cod.

———

Available now

SHADOW LANE III
The Romance of Discipline

Mischievous Susan Ross, now at Vassar, continues to exasperate Anthony Newton, while pursuing other dominant men. Heroically proportioned Michael Flagg proves capable but bossy, while handsome Marcus Gower has one too many demands. Dominating her girlfriend Diana brings Susan unexpected satisfaction, but playing top is work and so she turns her submissive over to the boys. Susan then inspires her adoring servant Dennis to revolt against his own submissive nature and turn his young mistress over his knee.

SHADOW LANE IV
The Chronicles of Random Point

Ever since the fifties, spanking has been practiced for the pleasure of adults in Random Point. The present era finds Hugo Sands at the center of its scene. Formerly a stern and imperious dom, his persistent love for Laura has all but civilized him. But instead of enchanting his favorite submissive, Hugo's sudden tameness has the opposite effect on Laura, who breaks every rule of their relationship to get him to behave like the strict martinet she once knew and loved. Meanwhile ivy league brat Susan Ross selects Sherman Cooper as the proper dominant to give her naughty friend Diana Stratton to and all the girls of Random Point conspire to rescue a delightful submissive from a cruel master.

SHADOW LANE V
The Spanking Persuasion

When Patricia's addiction to luxury necessitates a rescue from Hugo Sands, repayment is exacted in the form of discipline from one of the world's most implacable masters. Carter compels Aurora to give up her professional B&D lifestyle, not wholly through the use of a hairbrush. Marguerite takes a no-nonsense young husband, with predictable results. Sloan finds the girl of his dreams is more like the brat of his nightmares. Portia pushes Monty quite beyond control in trying to prove he's a switch. The stories are interconnected and share a theme: bad girls get spanked!

Available now

Images of Ironwood
by Don Winslow

Ironwood. The very name of that unique institution remains strongly evocative, even to this day. In this, the third volume of the famous Ironwood trilogy, the reader is once again invited to share in the Ironwood experience. *Images of Ironwood* presents selected scenes of unrelenting sensuality, of erotic longing, and occasionally, of those bizarre proclivities which touch the outer fringe of human sexuality.

In these pages we renew our acquaintance with James, the lusty entrepreneur who now directs the Ironwood enterprise; with his bevy of young female students being trained in the many ways of love; and with Cora Blasingdale, the cold remote mistress of discipline. The images presented here capture the essence of the Ironwood experience.

———

Available Now

Ironwood
by Don Winslow

The harsh reality of disinheritance and poverty vanish from the world of our young narrator, James, when he discovers he's in line for a choice position at an exclusive and very strict school for girls. Ironwood becomes for him a fantastic dream world where discipline knows few boundaries, and where his role as master affords him free reign with the willing, well-trained and submissive young beauties in his charge. As overseer of Ironwood, Cora Blasingdale is well-equipped to keep her charges in line. Under her guidance the saucy girls are put through their paces and tamed. And for James, it seems, life has just begun.

Order These Selected Blue Moon Titles

Souvenirs From a Boarding School $7.95	Shades of Singapore $7.95
The Captive $7.95	Images of Ironwood $7.95
Ironwood Revisited $7.95	What Love $7.95
Sundancer $7.95	Sabine $7.95
Julia $7.95	An English Education $7.95
The Captive II $7.95	The Encounter $7.95
Shadow Lane $7.95	Tutor's Bride $7.95
Belle Sauvage $7.95	A Brief Education $7.95
Shadow Lane III $7.95	Love Lessons $7.95
My Secret Life $9.95	Shogun's Agent $7.95
Our Scene $7.95	The Sign of the Scorpion $7.95
Chrysanthemum, Rose & the Samurai $7.95	Women of Gion $7.95
Captive V $7.95	Mariska I $7.95
Bombay Bound $7.95	Secret Talents $7.95
Sadopaideia $7.95	Beatrice $7.95
The New Story of O $7.95	S&M: The Last Taboo $8.95
Shadow Lane IV $7.95	"Frank" & I $7.95
Beauty in the Birch $7.95	Lament $7.95
Laura $7.95	The Boudoir $7.95
The Reckoning $7.95	The Bitch Witch $7.95
Ironwood Continued $7.95	Story of O $5.95
In a Mist $7.95	Romance of Lust $9.95
The Prussian Girls $7.95	Ironwood $7.95
Blue Velvet $7.95	Virtue's Rewards $5.95
Shadow Lane V $7.95	The Correct Sadist $7.95
Deep South $7.95	The New Olympia Reader $15.95

ORDER FORM
Attach a separate sheet for additional titles.

Title	Quantity	Price
_____	_____	_____
_____	_____	_____
_____	_____	_____
_____	_____	_____

Shipping and Handling (see charges below) _____

Sales tax (in CA and NY) _____

Total _____

Name _____

Address _____

City _____ State _____ Zip _____

Daytime telephone number _____

❑ Check   ❑ Money Order   (US dollars only. No COD orders accepted.)

Credit Card # _____ Exp. Date _____

❑ MC   ❑ VISA   ❑ AMEX

Signature _____

(if paying with a credit card you must sign this form.)

Shipping and Handling charges:*

Domestic: $4 for 1st book, $.75 each additional book. International: $5 for 1st book, $1 each additional book
*rates in effect at time of publication. Subject to Change.

Mail order to Publishers Group West, Attention: Order Dept., 1700 Fourth St., Berkeley, CA 94710,
or fax to (510) 528-3444.

PLEASE ALLOW 4-6 WEEKS FOR DELIVERY. ALL ORDERS SHIP VIA 4TH CLASS MAIL.